MURDER IN ALAMEDA

Kevin W. Luby

Cojamiba Publishing Company
Portland, OR

Murder In Alameda

ISBN 979-8-9901544-0-7 (eBook)
ISBN 979-8-9901544-1-4 (paperback)

Cover Photograph by Nicholas Steven
Cover Design by William Karb

Published by
Cojamiba Publishing Co.
Portland, OR
www.cojamiba.com

Acknowledgments

This novel is a sequel to *Murder in Bridge City*. That book was my first attempt at a murder mystery, and I really enjoyed creating the characters and the world they reside in. I enjoyed the process so much that I wanted to work with them, or at least most of them, again.

My hope is that the characters evolve and grow so that you, the reader, can better appreciate them and enjoy your visit to their world. The plan is to continue this series, with them evolving and aging with each new novel. Some characters will be mainstays, while others will come in and out of the series as necessary.

Amongst the many benefits of actually writing a novel is naming characters. I generally name them after friends. This is exactly what I did with this book. None of the fictional characters resemble their real selves, but, of course, I need to say that in order to avoid being sued. I thank these friends in advance for their forgiveness.

I also enjoy referencing local restaurants and coffee shops. I did not get any sort of kickback from any of these businesses. I just like supporting local businesses.

I want to thank Dan Addy for his assistance with teaching me how an anesthesiologist might kill someone in the operating room. All the information he provided me only cost me a beer and a copy of this book. Of course, such assistance will also terrify me next time I need a surgery.

King City Police Chief Ernie Happola provided me with some insight as to the inner workings of police departments. I, of course, took liberal literary license with the insight he provided me so blame me, not him, for any procedural errors.

Meghan Malone educated me on how counseling sessions really work. While her character's sessions with Bill Karb may not be particularly realistic, they are better than they would have been without her assistance.

As is my habit, I like to have an early draft of my books read by friends who are both literate and brutally honest. These sometimes-too-honest people include the lovely and talented Jane Kessel Luby, Ken Price, and Roger Boulden

Jane Kessel Luby has always been incredibly supportive of my writing endeavors. She has been so much more than just a wife—she truly is my best friend and confidante. She could have done much better than me and we both know it (although she graciously denies it). She is my inspiration for taking up writing murder mysteries.

My hope is that when I am long gone, my family, including grandchildren, will be proud of what I've published. This isn't about making money (although that would be nice); this is about making my family proud.

This book is dedicated to William Karb.
Bill passed well before his time and is missed.

This book is as always, and as ever,
dedicated to Conner Patrick Luby.
I was so lucky to have been his father for almost twenty-one years.

Finally, I dedicate this book and all of my love to my family
(Jane, Conner, Moira, Roger, Blake,
Remi, Jefferson, and Meghan),
all of whom have been incredibly patient, loving, and supportive.

Thank you all.

Contents

CHAPTER ONE

He heard her cellphone ringing downstairs in the kitchen. It was the sound of a duck quacking. For reasons that he never fully understood, that was her preferred ringtone. She thought it was cute; he thought it was just another annoying personality trait to be tolerated.

Looking at his watch, he noted that it was exactly 2:00 am. He turned over and lay on his back, his head slightly raised. Even from the other end of the hallway, he could hear her start to rustle and begin padding her way towards the landing. He knew she'd be able to see his door cracked open by the faint glow of the hallway's nightlight. That would keep her from turning on the hall light, as she wouldn't dare risk waking him up.

Her cellphone continued to ring or, more appropriately, quack.

He could sense her hesitate and then start rushing toward the stairs.

"Oh!"

Her cry of surprise was quickly followed by the sound of her tumbling down the steps. He counted eight thumps before it was quiet. Sitting up on his elbows, he strained to listen. At first there was nothing, only silence. Then he heard, very faintly, "Jim! Jim!"

Her cries sounded strained and then rapidly weakened.

He waited and noticed that her cellphone had stopped ringing. Quietly, he swung his legs to the side of the bed and stood up. He calmly put on his bathrobe, cinched the belt, and then walked to the top of the stairs. He looked down. In the faint light streaming in through the living room window, he could make out her still figure at the bottom of the staircase but couldn't tell if she was still alive or not.

Turning away from his wife, he walked to the guest bathroom and urinated. The flushing of the toilet seemed unnaturally loud to him. With the bathroom light still off, he washed his hands and dried them with the hand towel by the sink. He walked out of the dark room and into the not-quite-as-dark upstairs hallway. He stopped only briefly at the top of the stairs, reached down, and pulled at the duct tape and fishing line that was now cascading down the top of the stairs and bunched it up in his hand like a ball. He then placed it into the pocket of his bathrobe.

❧

The pain Charlene was feeling was sharp and searing. She couldn't seem to clear her head. She remembered hearing her cellphone ring and getting out of bed but nothing else. She could feel her cheek and the side of her head resting against something flat and hard.

Trying desperately to put the pieces together, she wondered if this was the hardwood floor at the bottom of the stairs. Is that what happened? Did she fall down the stairs? Was that it?

Opening her eyes, everything was a blur. Her vision was hampered by a warm liquid, stinging slightly. Even through the pain, she knew that it had to be blood. She reached her hand up to clear the liquid, but nothing happened. As much as she tried, it wouldn't move. In fact, she couldn't even feel her hand. There was just a void where the feeling of her hand, and even her whole arm, should be.

Fighting back the sense of panic, she tried to move her legs but couldn't feel them either. It was almost like they weren't there at all. The pain, such as it was, seemed mostly focused on her head.

"Jim! Jim!"

Her voice was strained and, try as she might, she couldn't get out anything but a hoarse croak. Through the red film covering her eyes, she saw someone walking toward her. The figure almost seemed to be floating.

"Jim, help me," she mouthed but no sound other than a guttural moan escaped her lips. Again, she tried to reach out but, no matter how she struggled, she couldn't move. The figure loomed over her, and she felt a hand pinch her nostrils shut and then another hand cover her mouth. Both hands were smooth, warm, and familiar. "Funny," she thought briefly, "this is what I notice?"

She struggled to breathe, but couldn't. Then the hands relaxed slightly, and she took a complete inhale and then exhaled. She tried to calm herself. Before she could inhale again, the hands clamped down once more. She could feel a burning pressure at the top of her lungs and an urge to cough but couldn't push the air through the hands.

The pain started to recede at the same rate as the panic took complete and total hold of her. She strained to shake off the hands, but her body refused to cooperate. She stared into the dark eyes floating above her. The blackness on the edges of her blurred vision began to grow larger. At this point, her vision was little more than a pinhole, but it was enough for her to recognize the eyes staring back at her.

The thought that sprung to mind was simply, "Why?"

After what seemed to her like minutes but was only seconds, the blackness consumed her completely. She saw a final blaze of bright light and had one last thought—so this is what it feels like to die.

He looked at his watch. It was 2:12 am. He reached down to feel the side of her neck, looking for a pulse. There was none. He reached for her wrist and still, nothing. He let her hand drop to the floor.

Dr. J. Matthew Davies climbed back up the stairs and down the hall to his bedroom. He lay down on the soft mattress, pulled the covers up, and, within fifteen minutes, was sound asleep again. He only jumped slightly when the alarm went off at 5:35 am.

Chapter Two

Reaching out her hand, she said, "Good morning, Mr. Karb. I'm Dr. Meghan Malone."

"Nice to meet you," he replied, his voice flat and guarded.

"May we dispense with the formalities?" she asked. "May I call you Bill and have you just call me Meghan?"

"Sure."

He sat down at the chair she'd motioned to and crossed his right ankle over his left knee. A thousand thoughts were going through his mind, most concerning questions of how he got here. Karb hated talking about himself and the idea of therapy in general. Nonetheless, here he was.

He looked around. The office was functional but not elegant in a downtown building that was past its prime but still well-appointed. The walls were painted an off-white, and her desk was modern, a mix of chrome and maple. It wasn't cheap but it also wasn't flashy. There were no diplomas behind her desk or elsewhere. The pictures on the wall were mostly abstract. The white shutters covered only the bottom half of the windows, allowing privacy without making the office too dark. Through the slats of the shutters, he could see some of the trees at street level just starting to turn the bright green of spring.

Dr. Malone was either successful and didn't care about the trappings of success or she was still working her way up the food chain of the psychology industry. Given her age, it was more likely the latter, but either way it didn't matter to him.

She looked to be in her mid- to late-thirties, with dark brown hair and a slightly pale complexion. Her hair was pulled back in a tight ponytail. She wore a trim gray plaid jacket and skirt, with the top button of her dark blue shirt undone. Her clothes were sufficient to let people know she was a woman, but not sufficient to allow anyone, or at least most people, to get a sense of her sexuality.

A small gold chain adorned her neck. He couldn't see what, if any, pendant it might hold up. There was no wedding ring or other jewelry to be seen. A pair of reading glasses hung on a dark beaded chain around her neck. This was a professional setting, and she was appropriately and professionally attired.

Dr. Malone settled down in the chair across from Karb and stared at him. Without looking, she picked up a pad of legal paper and pulled a pen out of her jacket.

"So, what can I do for you, Bill?"

"Doc, that's for you to figure out. You know why I'm here."

"I *do* know why you're here, Bill. Your captain has ordered you to get some mental health counseling. He's already removed you, at least temporarily, from active duty and has you doing just paperwork. That's it, isn't it?"

"Pretty much," Karb responded, a tinge of anger showed in his voice.

"Given that, you *know* what I can do for you. I can either help you or not. If I do, you return to your full duties as a detective. If I'm not successful, you don't return to full duties and may actually proceed to a full discharge for disability. That seems pretty simple to me. How does it seem to you?"

Karb took a moment to really look at the eyes of the psychologist in front of him. She obviously was sharper than he had initially surmised. He told himself that he knew better than to do that. As a detective, one should never make assumptions solely based on a person's age, the way they look, or how they dress. He recognized that his emotions were on edge, and this is what caused the initial miscalculation. His dislike of being at a therapist's office, and his general disdain of mental health counseling as a whole, had led him to infer she was something less than what she obviously was.

"Yeah, it seems pretty simple. So, how do we proceed? You want me to tell you my life story? Do you want me to tell you about my relationship with my father?"

Dr. Malone looked down and shook her head. After a moment, she looked up and leaned forward a little. "Bill, let's not play games. Neither one of us has time for that, or quite frankly, any interest in that. I'll make a deal with you. I'll be completely honest with you if you'll be similarly honest with me. Is that fair?"

"Yeah," he said, looking down at his hands.

"Okay, so no bullshit?"

The use of a curse word surprised Karb but, still not looking up, he nodded his head slightly up and down. "Sure."

"Before we really begin, I want to remind you that whatever we talk about is completely confidential. Under Oregon law, there is complete confidentiality between us with only a couple of exceptions."

Karb spoke up, "Yeah, unless I tell you that I intend to hurt someone or hurt myself. That right?"

"Yes, Bill, that's right. Okay then, you don't have to tell me your whole life story. I've got the basics down pretty well. I listened to your interviews with Meg Nguyen for her podcast—pretty compelling stuff. She even let me listen to the unedited tapes—all of them, so I could get a better feel for you.

"I listened to them twice, all twelve hours of them. I also talked to your captain. He told me how you were a leading suspect in the death of Scott Sorochak, the man who killed your wife and unborn son, but that you alibied out. I'm not sure he was convinced by your alibi, but he wasn't ready to push it any further.

"He seems to think that you're a damn fine detective—his words, not mine—but is concerned that you are a ticking time bomb. Again, his words, not mine."

Dr. Malone paused for a moment and stared at Karb. She bit her lip just slightly.

"So, Bill, are you a ticking time bomb?"

Karb let out a long sigh and rubbed his face with his hands. "Doc, look, I get that I may be some textbook nutjob to you, but all I want to do is get back to my job. What do we have to do so I can do that?"

Dr. Malone wrote some notes on her pad, keeping it at a sufficient angle so he couldn't see what she was writing.

"Let's not get ahead of ourselves. For counseling to be truly effective, we need to build a certain amount of trust. You need to be able to talk to me and I need to believe you are being honest with me. This is more than just no bullshit. We need to figure out how you got here, where you need to go, and how to get you there."

She noticed that he was fidgeting slightly. He also seemed to recognize what he was doing and stilled himself. He looked up but not at her. He was looking over her left shoulder. Meghan Malone had once lived in New York and recognized that this tactic allowed someone to appear confident but not threatening. Locking eyes with someone could be deemed an act of aggression and could create a confrontation. Looking down was often a sign of weakness and, similarly, could trigger an unpleasant event. She knew that by just looking over someone's shoulder, she would still be looking up, giving an appearance of confidence but not aggression.

"Bill, look at me."

Karb shifted his gaze slightly to look directly at her.

"Good. Would you like to tell me what happened with Sorochak?"

He paused and stared at her. She stared right back, not breaking his gaze.

"No."

"Okay, that will be something we'll address down the line. The man who killed your wife Janice and your unborn son dies, under mysterious circumstances, on his first night out of prison. You have an alibi, but no one is completely convinced. This is but one of the red flags that everyone, and not just me, sees. Your best friend and fellow detective, Mike Kelley, is also suspected but, similarly, he alibis out although, again, no one is completely convinced.

"Bill, just remember, we're going to talk about that eventually… just not today. We will definitely talk about this in great detail."

Dr. Malone stopped, frowned, and wrote some more notes on her pad. For reasons he couldn't articulate if he was asked, this bothered him.

"Let's get some more background on you, information that Meg's interview with you didn't fully address. Are your parents still alive?"

"No."

"What happened to them?"

"My folks got in a car accident when I was young. My father died instantly; my mom was seriously injured but stayed alive until I was eighteen."

"How seriously was she injured?"

"She broke her back at L1-L2. She was a paraplegic."

"Any siblings?"

"No."

"Any other family in the area?"

"No."

Dr. Malone let out a quiet sigh. "So, you took care of your mom?"

Karb merely nodded his head.

"How old were you, Bill, when the accident occurred?

"Ten."

"That's a lot of responsibility for a ten-year-old boy."

"You do what you have to do."

"And your mom lived another eight years?"

"Give or take."

Dr. Malone quickly looked at her watch and then looked at Karb. She saw a man who had been battered by life but still functioned…mostly. This was a man who was forced to become an adult well before he should have and then had to deal with the murder of his wife and unborn son. On top of that, his best friend and fellow suspect in the death of Scott Sorochak then moves away under what could best be described as curious circumstances.

She knew that this was going to take a lot of work and that she was going to have to probe very carefully, gently, and slowly. Despite his outward appearance, she believed him to be incredibly fragile, even if he wasn't aware of it.

"Why is it so important to get back to work?"

"Because that's what I do. I'm a detective, a *damn good detective* as you just said, and I've got work to do."

"Okay, I get it."

She stared at him, and he could tell that she was thinking but he couldn't be sure what about. She had to gain his trust and an idea came to her.

"Bill, I've got another deal for you." She saw his ears perk up slightly and his eyes widen slowly.

"I'll authorize your return to full duty…"

Karb sat up straight.

"…if you agree to meet with me once a week."

"For how long?"

"For as long as it takes…for as long as *I say* it takes. Also, we're going to talk about some very difficult issues, and you won't be able to just refuse to talk about it. We're going to talk about Sorochak…eventually; we're going to talk about what happened with Mike Kelley…eventually; we're going to talk about your family…eventually. My goal is to help you somehow have a life that involves more than just your job. Do we have a deal?"

"Yeah," Karb said without hesitation. Having to open up about things in the past would be something to worry about in the future. Now was an opportunity to get back to work.

"When can I go back to full duty?"

"I'll get the paperwork over to your captain this afternoon."

It looked to her almost as if Karb smiled at that, but she couldn't be sure.

"Bill, one last thing. I'm going to have to have periodic conversations with Captain Schnadig, but it will only be as to your general condition, how you are participating in, and responding to, our counseling sessions, and how you are handling your workload. I will not disclose any specifics that you share with me."

She looked at him but couldn't read any response on his face.

"Do you understand what I'm saying?"

"Yeah, I get it."

"As long as you hold up your end of the bargain and attend, and fully participate, in these sessions in good faith, there should be no problem…unless I start seeing that your continued work as a detective becomes a risk to you or anyone else. Is that fair?"

"Sure, Doc, that's fair. Can I go now?"

Dr. Malone picked up a leather-bound book off to the side of her desk and started flipping through the pages.

"How about every Wednesday at 3:00 pm. Will that work for you?"

"Do I have a choice?" Karb's voice was more resignation than resentment.

Dr. Malone smiled and responded, "Not really, at least not so long as you want to remain a detective."

Karb nodded, stood up, and said, "Thanks, Doc. I'll see you next week."

She looked up briefly and then looked down again and began writing her notes. After he closed the door behind him, she picked up her dictation recorder and started going through that first appointment, only rarely looking at her notes. The dictation would be transcribed and kept in Karb's folder in her computer, along with her handwritten notes after they were scanned.

Dr. Malone could only hope that the folder would become voluminous as that would indicate that Karb was, in fact, holding up his end of the bargain and they were making progress. She was optimistic, but not confident, that that would happen. He was going to be a challenge like no other she had experienced, but she was looking forward to it.

❧

CHAPTER THREE

"Nine-One-One. Police or Fire?"

"I need help! My wife, I just found her at the bottom of the stairs. She's dead. I don't know what happened. She has no pulse. Help! I need some help."

"Calm down, sir. You're calling on a cellphone so the first thing I need is your address."

"Uh, uh, uh…get an ambulance. Please! Please!"

"Sir, I'll have one there right away, but I need your address. Sir?

"It's…uh, uh, uh…3028 NE Alameda Street. Please hurry. Should I have checked for a pulse? Should I have touched her? What should I…"

"Sir, we've got an ambulance on the way. It will be there in just a couple of minutes. Is she moving at all?"

"No…well, no, she's dead. I checked her pulse. I'm a doctor and she's cold to the touch. Oh my God, what should I do? Is someone on their way?"

"Sir, I've got an ambulance crew only minutes away. Can you unlock the door for them?"

"Yeah…um…um…is someone on their way? What am I going to do? Is someone coming?"

"Yes, sir, they are, but I need you to unlock your front door first. The EMTs will be there any second and they need to get to her as quickly as possible."

"Of course, of course…I just…just…"

"Sir, I know how difficult this is, but I need you to take a breath and make sure you do what I say. Can you do that? You said you're a doctor, right? What's your name?"

"Yes, it's Davies. Dr. James Davies. I'm an anesthesiologist."

"OK, Dr. Davies. Are you unlocking the front door?"

"Uhm, yeah, yeah. I just had to step over her. She looks gray. Oh my god, what am I going to do?"

"Mr. Davies, have you unlocked the front door?"

"I'm doing that now. What? The door is already unlocked. That's so odd. Could someone have…oh god, my poor Charlene."

Davies could hear the ambulance now. He took a deep breath and bent down to check her pulse again. He had to be certain. Her skin was still cold to the touch and there was no suggestion of a heartbeat.

Hearing the ambulance getting closer, he dropped the phone and kicked it across the hardwood floor. He yelled, "Oh crap, wait a minute…I dropped the phone."

Rather than heading across the room to the phone, he sprinted up to the top of the stairs. Davies looked down at the baseboard and ran his finger across where the tape had been. There was still a slight bit of adhesive. As he was about to try rubbing it off, he saw the flashing of the ambulance lights splay across the walls.

"Dr. Davies? Are you still there?" He could faintly hear the 911 operator's voice over his phone as he rushed down the stairs and across the room.

'Yes! Yes, I'm here…I'm just…I guess I…"

He looked through the window beside the front door and saw the ambulance pulling into the driveway. He picked the phone back up. "I'm back, sorry, I…wait, I see the ambulance."

He walked towards the front door but, before opening it, he took one last look at his wife. Charlene was lying on her back at the bottom of the stairs. Her legs were twisted and partially on the first step up. She had one arm on her side and the other contorted behind her back. Her head was facing him, but at an odd angle, and her eyes were open. Dry blood covered much of her face. He reached for the doorknob, flinging the door open and called out, "Quick! Quick. My wife is over here!"

He absently placed the phone in the pocket of his bathrobe and could faintly hear the emergency operator calling out, "Dr. Davies! Dr. Davies! Are you still there?"

The first EMT through the door immediately looked to his left, where Davies was pointing, and then to his right where he saw the crumpled body of a thin woman in a pink satin robe. He rushed over to her, felt her cheek as he bent over to see if he could hear any breathing. There was nothing. He reached for her wrist to take her pulse. Still nothing. He could hear his partner talking to the husband but tried to keep his focus on the dead woman lying in front of him.

He brushed her light blond hair aside, some of it sticking to the dried blood. Giving the appearance of checking her carotid artery for a pulse, he actually examined her for signs of any bruising around her neck. In his experience, people did sometimes just fall down the stairs but, far too often, they were pushed as the result of a physical altercation. Evidence of such was often in the form of bruising around the neck from choking. He found nothing there, but he did notice bruising on the outside of her right arm, as well as contusions to her right knee and left cheek.

The bruises on the upper arm consisted of four small, round, lightly purple marks with yellowing along the edges. He lightly placed the four fingertips of his right hand over the marks, and they matched. The EMT made a mental note to mention it to both the police when they arrived and to the ME, as the bruises were consistent with being roughly grabbed. He'd seen those types of bruises many times before in domestic violence cases. These looked recent.

Grabbing a white sheet from the gurney, he placed it over the woman. As he stood back up, he heard a car pull into the driveway outside. The EMT walked to the front door and watched as a Portland police cruiser pulled in beside the ambulance. A young policeman stepped out and quickly ran to the front door.

"What ya got?" the officer asked.

"Deceased, middle-aged female. It appears she died when she fell down the stairs, likely a broken neck and possible back. I can't tell if she fell or was pushed but I did note some bruises on her arm that would be consistent with DV. The husband is in the living room with my partner."

"Is she questioning him?"

"No, no, nothing like that. Rosie hasn't been hardened by the job yet. She still finds time to comfort people. They're in the living room.

"When you talk to the husband, you might want to ask why it took him so long to find the body. When I got here, it was obvious she'd been there for a number of hours."

"Got it. Okay, I'll go in and talk to him. Do you have a name for the vic?"

"Nope, sorry. Rosie should have it though."

With that, both men walked into the house. The EMT adjusted the white sheet covering the body and then went outside to smoke a cigarette.

Officer Sprehe glanced at the body at the bottom of the stairs and then took a quick look up. It was fairly dark on the landing, but nothing looked unusual. The stair treads appeared to be either cherry or hemlock. The handrail was dark twisted wrought iron.

He then gazed across the lavish home and saw a middle-aged man in the living room sitting on an ornately embroidered sofa and talking to the other EMT. Sprehe took a quick inventory of what he could see of the house from where he stood. It was clearly large. The furnishings appeared expensive, even if a little too gaudy for his tastes. The Persian rug in the entry way looked authentic and the rug in the living room was the whitest he'd ever seen. He wondered, for a moment, whether he should take off his shoes but decided against it.

Sprehe looked at the husband sitting, hunched over and holding his stomach, on the sofa. He was rocking back and forth. The female EMT was on the left and leaning into the man, quietly talking to him, with her hand on his knee. The man looked to be in his early- to mid-fifties and was wearing a crimson silk bathrobe with black pajama bottoms sticking out from beneath the robe. He had a pair of leather slippers on his feet.

He was thin and of medium height. His hair was longer than you'd see on most men his age and was both thinning and disheveled. The word "bedhead" sprung to mind.

"Dr. Davies, can I get you some coffee or even just some water?" he heard the EMT ask.

The man looked up and Sprehe could see that his eyes appeared to be red. "Yes, please, water would be nice. She's dead, isn't she?"

The EMT nodded her head and then noticed the officer in the doorway.

Sprehe walked up to the two. "Good morning, sir. My name is Officer Tim Sprehe with the Portland Police Department."

The man stood up quickly and looked startled. He swayed unsteadily.

"Am I under arrest? Do you think I killed her? I didn't, I swear, I didn't."

The EMT stood up and put her hand on the man's elbow, he appeared to be on the edge of outright panic. She slowly spoke into his ear, "Dr. Davies, the officer just has to ask you some questions.

This is all standard procedure. No one is accusing you of doing anything wrong. Isn't that right, Officer?"

Sprehe looked at the EMT. She was in her late twenties, tall, attractive, and clearly comfortable in this situation.

"That's right, I just have to ask some questions so I will be able to report what happened."

This seemed to calm the man and he sat back down.

"I am Dr. James Davies. That is my wife, Charlene," he said, nodding in the direction of the stairs. "What do you want to know?"

The man appeared to Sprehe to be completely exhausted. The officer nodded to the EMT that she could leave now. He couldn't help but watch her walk out the front door.

"Mr. Davies…"

"It's *Dr.* Davies."

Sprehe started again. "Absolutely, I apologize. *Dr.* Davies, what do you think happened?"

"Of course, of course. Well, I got up this morning and…I'm sorry, do you mind if I go to the bathroom? I haven't gone yet this morning and I am very uncomfortable."

"Yes, sir, of course. I'll wait here."

Dr. Davies stood up and, again, appeared to be somewhat unsteady on his feet. Suddenly he reached into the pocket of his bathrobe to pick up the cellphone he had put there. The 911 operator was still on the line. As he pulled the phone out of his pocket, the officer saw a ball of what looked like string and duct tape fall to the floor.

Flustered, Dr. Davies quickly reached down to grab the ball and stuff it back into the pocket of his robe. He looked down at the phone, pushed the button ending the phone call, turned, and started to quickly walk away towards the rear of the house.

"Dr. Davies…what was that? Can I see what fell out of your pocket?"

As he quickly shuffled away, Davies called out, "I'm sorry…I think I'm going to be sick."

He then raced over to a door by the kitchen, hunched over at the waist, and walked into what Sprehe assumed was a downstairs bathroom. Davies shut the door behind him and Sprehe heard the click of a lock. Standing outside of the bathroom door, he could hear the water being turned on. Looking around, Sprehe quickly walked across the living room and over to the stairway, carefully stepped over the body, and sprinted up the stairs. At the top, he looked around the landing and down at the body. He then bent down and ran his fingers across the lower walls and baseboards just above the steps. He felt something sticky on the baseboard on the outer wall and took his phone out to try and take a picture.

Officer Sprehe heard the toilet flush downstairs and quickly walked down the stairs and back into the living room. He saw Dr. Davies walk out of the bathroom, his face flushed. Davies walked back to the sofa and sat down.

"Dr. Davies, can I see what fell out of your pocket just a few moments ago?"

"Oh, it was just some tissue. I have a nasal condition and always have tissues in my pockets."

"Can I see it, please?"

"Of course," he responded and reached into his pocket, pulling out a wad of tissue paper.

"Dr. Davies, that is not what I saw fall out of your pocket."

Davies looked away. "I'm sorry, I don't know what you're talking about. This is all I have in my pocket."

Sprehe stood there for a while and just stared at the man in front of him. He was starting to suspect that the death of this woman was not an accident, but needed to tread very carefully.

"Okay, sir. Do you mind if I take a look around the house?"

"Oh, I'd rather you not…at least not right now. I need a moment and then I have to call Charlene's daughter. Can this wait until tomorrow?"

"Doctor, it's pretty important that I look around the house, if for no reason than to confirm that this isn't a crime scene."

Davies snapped his head up. "A crime scene? You think I killed my wife? Is that what you think?"

His voice was becoming both higher in pitch and louder in volume. Davies appeared to be on the edge of hysteria.

"Let me tell you something, young man. I adored my wife and would never hurt her. You accusing me of having something to do with her death is just disgusting. I think that you better leave right now. If you want to talk to me again or if you want to snoop around the house, you can damn well talk to my lawyer. Now get the hell out of here!" Dr. Davies' voice was nearly a shout.

Sprehe lowered his voice in an attempt to calm him down. "Sir, I haven't accused you of anything and I apologize if I led you to believe otherwise. It's just that I have a job to do and part of that job is to conduct a basic investigation when, and where, a person dies. It's not my job to make any determination as to the cause of death, but Oregon law says that I control the scene…your house. All I'm asking is to take a brief look around. I can do it anyway, but I'd rather have your consent. Again, my job is to just observe and then pass my observations on to my superiors. I'm going to call in the medical examiner now to come out. He'll make the initial determination as to what happens next."

"Well, thank you, young man, for your apology but I still don't feel comfortable with you snooping around my house. I want you to go now. You can make arrangements to come back sometime later. My wife has a lot of valuable jewelry, and I would feel better if someone were here when you go through the house."

Sprehe noted that Dr. Davies' level of agitation was considerably lower than just a few moments before. He was now calm and collected and this only caused the officer more concern. He wasn't used to people experiencing such a wide fluctuation of emotions in such a short period of time.

"Again, Doctor, under Oregon law, I have control of the house right now while we do an initial investigation. I'll call the medical examiner now and once he comes out and makes his determination, we can leave. Until then, the EMTs can't take your wife away. There is a process that needs to be followed."

Davies stared at him, but Sprehe was having difficulty figuring out what he might be thinking.

Sprehe continued, "I realize that this is unsettling and the sooner I take a look around, the sooner we can be out of your hair, and we can all move on."

"I'm sorry, officer, but you'll just have to wait. As I said, my wife has a lot of jewelry…" His voice trailed off as he looked over the officer's shoulder and saw that the EMTs had come back, pushing a gurney towards his wife's body. They didn't, however, put her on the gurney, but rather, just stood there and seemed almost to be guarding her body.

"Please go now so I can call my step-daughter and start making arrangements."

Shaking his head, the young officer responded, "Dr. Davies, I'm going to step outside and call the medical examiner. When he arrives, he and I will come back in and complete our initial investigation. If you have a concern about this, I recommend that you call an attorney as this *is* going to happen and it's going to happen this morning. I'll let you know when the ME gets here. Until then, I'm going to have the EMTs stay here. Do you understand?"

Davies looked at the officer and then he seemed to just sag and slump down onto the sofa. He placed his head in his hands and Officer Sprehe could hear him muttering to himself.

The officer then walked towards the front door, quietly whispered into the male EMT's ear, and then walked outside and stood beside his cruiser. He first radioed into the station and then called the ME's office and requested an immediate site visit.

While this was going on, Sprehe took a close look at the house and the surrounding neighborhood. The neighbors, in various states of morning dress, were standing on their front lawns in groups of three to five, staring at him. He chose not to acknowledge them, as to do so might encourage them to come over and ask questions.

After ten minutes, he decided to return to the interior of the house and wait for the ME.

❧

Chapter Four

Meg stared at the cold bottle of Sessions Lager in her hand. It was a little early for a drink, but it tasted great. It was an unseasonably warm April afternoon and the patio at the Tin Shed Garden Café was crowded. She was sitting at a table for four and tried, unsuccessfully, to stop looking at her watch. She had never been one for waiting patiently and even less of the type of person who could accept people being late. She looked at her watch…again. It was 12:06 pm.

The Tin Shed was one of her favorite lunch spots. It was quirky and dog friendly and just so stereotypically Portland—the murals on the wall, the colorful table umbrellas, and the self-service water jugs. The food was mostly breakfast and lunch fare and included some great vegetarian options. She smiled at a Weimaraner that was staring intently at her.

It was too trendy for some of her contacts but was just right for this meeting. She looked at her watch again—12:08 pm.

"Meg!"

The voice came from out on the sidewalk, and she looked up to see detectives Debbie Pedersen and Carol Capobianco. Pedersen was waving and Meg could see that Capobianco had a phone to her ear as she stepped out of the car.

"Sorry for being late," Pedersen said. "Oh good, you've already got a beer. Damn, that looks good."

"Do you want me to order a couple for the two of you?"

Capobianco held up her index finger as she continued talking into her phone. Pedersen replied, "No, we're still on the clock."

The server walked by, and Pedersen said, "Two ice teas please, both with lemon. Also, can we get a couple of packets of Stevia?"

The server nodded her head and the two detectives sat down, with Capobianco finishing up her call and placing her phone in her purse.

"I'm really sorry, Meg. You know how it is."

Meg smiled and took a sip of her beer.

Capobianco continued, "So fill us in. How's it feel to be a network star and why are you slumming with us back here in Portland?"

Through a sad smile, Meg responded, "Well, it's a long story but the gist is that I quit."

Both detectives stared at her, Pedersen's mouth slightly agape.

"You quit *20/20*? What the hell?" Capobianco said in a voice loud enough to cause the people at other tables to look up and over at them.

"I thought that was your dream job. What happened?" Pedersen asked in a noticeably quieter voice than her partner's.

"The problem was me. I finally figured out that I'm just not a very good employee."

"But, Meg, this was *20/20*. I saw that episode you did on the child killer out of Seattle. You knocked it out of the park."

"Yeah, but it's different than when I'm doing my podcast. When I do that, I'm in charge. I get to decide what cases to talk about and how to present them. I write the copy and just have someone to lend a hand and help with the recording and some of the editing. It's stressful but it's all mine. With *20/20*, I worked with a producer and production assistants who do much of the footwork and craft the story. I had fact checkers and interns. My script got written and rewritten until I didn't even recognize my own writing. We'd get notes from the network about how I spoke and what my hair looked like and what color suit looked best on me. It…well, it just wasn't me. That's not how I work best. It's not how I *like* to work. I need to be more than just a talking head. I've got a lot of respect for the other on-air talent but I'm not like them. I'm better, and frankly happier, when I can do *what* I want *how* I want."

Pedersen reached over and placed her hand over Nguyen's forearm. "Meg, I understand, and I think I speak for both of us when I say that we fully support your decision. Isn't that right, Capo?"

Capobianco nodded her head but, from the look on her face, Nguyen could tell that she didn't really understand. Some people are able to work for others and be happy and some people can't. Capobianco's background in the military and then the police force didn't lend itself to the concept of working independently. She was happy to work for others, be part of a bureaucracy, and let others deal with the stresses of management.

Meg had come to realize that she was just one of those who craved independence and self-reliance. She didn't want to have to ask someone else's permission. It was a life of stress, but Meg always seemed to be able to handle that, although perhaps not always in the healthiest of fashions. More importantly, it was a life of opportunity, knowing she could pack it up and disappear at any time. She lived simply so didn't need to make a lot of money. She'd saved most of her salary from her short stint with *20/20* and that would hold her for a bit.

Just then, the server came by and placed ice teas in front of the two detectives. "Will you be ordering lunch today, ladies?"

Nguyen looked across the table at her companions and raised an eyebrow. Capobianco shook her head no.

"No, I think we're just going to have a drink and catch up. Thank you though."

"My pleasure." The server, a twentyish woman with short hair and a plethora of tattoos, stopped and then leaned slightly towards Nguyen, "Can I just say, I'm a big fan."

"Thank you very much. That is very nice to hear."

The server smiled at Meg and then walked away.

"Well, this makes a perfect segue into why I asked you two out today."

Capobianco immediately said, "You're looking for a new story."

"Capo, be nice."

"No, Debbie, she's right. I've been reading *The Oregonian* and the *Willamette Week,* as well as the websites for the local radio and television stations, but haven't seen anything of interest. What are you working on?"

Capobianco spoke first. "Nothing particularly interesting. Debbie's got a grand jury next week on a bungled robbery case and I've got a road rage case I'm working on. Neither is particularly suitable for your podcast."

Capobianco then stopped and looked briefly at her partner before turning back to Nguyen.

"Even if we had something Meg, the captain has made it abundantly clear that he was very unhappy with our helping you in the past."

"But I thought I did a pretty good job with the Karb series. That should have earned me some goodwill with him."

"Oh, you did a great job with that. I'm still amazed that Karb participated and that's part of the problem. With the whole crap about a possible serial killer and the possible involvement of Karb and Kelley…well, you ruffled more than a few feathers.

"The brass still doesn't like that they don't know the whole story. If Kelley were still here, there probably would have been a more extensive IA investigation. As it is, there are just too many questions and too few answers. They think you know more than you let on."

"So, I'm a little hot right now?"

"Yeah, not as much as you were before you left for New York, but once the captain finds out you're back in town, I'm sure we'll get our marching orders to avoid you like the plague."

"Well, that kind of sucks."

The two detectives looked at one another again and Pedersen spoke softly, "Look, Meg. If we hear of anything, we'll still give you a heads up. We probably won't be able to give you any updates, but we should be able to alert you if we hear of anything that might be right for you. Capo, do you agree?"

"Sure, but I'm close enough to retirement to not want to take *too* much of a risk in pissing off the captain. I think, however, that we're safe in letting you know about the early stages of any investigation that might be of interest."

"How many years do you have left?"

Capobianco responded, "Last time I checked, it was seven years, one hundred and eight days and…" she looked at her watch, "about four and a half hours, but that's just an estimate."

They all laughed at that.

"How about you, Debbie? How much longer do you have?"

"I took quite a bit of maternity leave and PTO over the years, so I've still got another nine plus years."

"Alright, I get it. Is it safe to assume that there's nothing going on right now that you could tell me about?"

"Meg," Capobianco said, "there's nothing going on, regardless of whether we could tell you about it or not. There's still enough serious crime out there but nothing particularly juicy."

Looking down at her watch, Capobianco jerked her head up and said, "Oh crap, we've got to go."

"Really? Are you sure I can't buy you lunch?"

"Sorry, Meg, next time. You picking up the tab for our ice teas is more than enough. If you're not working right now, you've got some time to relax. So stay and have a good lunch. I've heard the Heartless Artichoke Sandwich is pretty good."

Meg chuckled and merely said, "It is, but I'll probably pass. I've got to start turning over some rocks." She stood up and hugged both of the detectives. "It was really nice to see you both again. If you hear of anything, please let me know. It's only a matter of time before I peek through the right blinds and discover some dirty deeds out there. If I find anything, I'll let you know…just as a sign of *my* good faith."

"And to try and build some goodwill back with the department?" Capobianco asked.

Meg merely smiled as the two women finished their ice teas and walked away.

Once they were out of earshot, Meg softly said, "Fuck!" She walked into the café to pay the bill.

CHAPTER FIVE

Karb knocked on the door. Almost immediately, he heard the captain say, "Come in."

Slowly opening the door, Karb looked in at the intentionally dark office. The building that housed the Portland Police Department and the jail was relatively modern, being less than ten years old, and had lots of windows to allow for sunlight both in the offices and the internal areas. The captain, however, always kept the blinds on his windows mostly closed. If asked, he'd say that he didn't want to be distracted by the weather, but the truth was that he was better able to concentrate in the darkness. Also, it matched his general mood.

His desk was overflowing with files and the captain himself looked tired. Even though it was only 7:45 a.m., he looked like he hadn't slept in a couple of days.

"Sit down, Bill."

Karb walked over to one of the wooden chairs in front of the desk and sat down. He clasped his hands on his lap and waited.

Captain Schnadig looked at Karb and took a deep breath. "You know I don't like this."

"I know, sir."

"Fuck, Bill, there was a reason I put you on desk duty. You're a wreck. You've been a wreck for years but these last thirteen months…well, that has been something else altogether."

"Yes, sir."

The captain stood up and walked over to his window, pushing the blinds to one side to peer out at the Willamette River. Karb stood up and, from a distance, looked over the captain's shoulder. Even on gray and rainy days like today, the river still ran and allowed a person to get lost in the flow. A log slowly floated along the river; a bird perched atop it.

Back when their friendship had been better, the captain told Karb how he enjoyed staring at the river but had to fight the urge to get lost in the flow.

Without turning around, the captain asked, "How did you convince her to recommend you get back to active duty?"

Karb sat back down and spoke to his back. "To tell you the truth, sir, I don't know. I think I was honest with her and that's something…well, that's something I haven't done with anyone in a long time…probably not even myself. I realize there have been problems but…"

The captain spun around, his face rapidly growing red. "Problems, Bill? Problems? For Christ's sake, that whole debacle with Sorochak was a catastrophe. I know you alibied out of his killing, but I don't buy it. The day he gets released, he jumps out a window? Yeah, that makes no sense."

"Sir…"

The captain put his hand out, emphatically motioning for Karb to stop talking. Walking back to his chair, he tried to slow his breath and take control of his emotions.

"Since Kelley left, you've scared off three partners. No one wants to work with you, Bill. The DA's office doesn't trust you. I've been trying to steer you away from any cases that might involve you testifying in Court because I have absolutely no confidence that you could withstand cross-examination. What good are you to me if I can't rely upon you? Every day, *every…fucking…day*," the captain practically spit out the words, "I expect to get a phone call that you've blown your brains out. Seriously, Bill, every single day!"

Karb sat and listened, taking deep breaths to maintain his composure. He was, by nature, a fighter, but now was not the time to argue or stand up to his boss.

"Ian," he said in a calm voice, "I'm still a good detective and I'm trying. The shrink? She surprised me. More importantly, I finally figured out that she might be my last chance. I don't like talking about myself, but I really don't have much choice, do I?"

"No, Bill, you don't. You and I go back a long way but what has been going on over the last year or so…fuck over the last several years…I can't let that continue. I can't let you destroy this department."

Now it was Karb's turn to stand up and walk over to the window. Pulling aside the blinds, Karb looked past the river and toward the West Hills. The fog was clinging to the upper reaches, and he knew there were million-dollar houses hidden there. He envied them, being able to hide themselves in the fog. That, almost more than anything else, is where he wanted to be—hidden in the fog, his emotions blanketed by the mist for no one to see.

Without turning around, he started "Ian, I know I've run out of favors. All I'm asking is this one more chance. Just one more, for good or bad, this is my life. I'm at least acknowledging a problem and that's not something I would have done even a week ago."

The captain nodded his head in agreement. Karb couldn't see the nod but took his silence as having the same effect.

Turning around and facing his old friend and with a voice that was strained, he said, "Give me just this one last chance… please. Either I'll get my shit together or I'm gone. Hell, I won't even make you fire me if I screw up again."

Captain Schnadig stood up and walked over to Karb. "I can't give you another partner."

"That's okay, I can work alone."

"No, Bill, you can't work alone. I can't rely upon you with a serious investigation all by yourself, not at this point. The DA's office has told me that they won't prosecute a case of yours if you are going to be on the stand. As I said, they don't trust you. I'm going to team you up with Capo and Pedersen. You'll work with them for the next couple of months."

The captain looked down and absently picked up a file from the corner of his desk. Absently shifting the file in his hands, almost seeming to weigh it, he continued, "You've got seniority on them, but they are the leads on any and all investigations going forward. Understand?"

"Yes, sir, but for how long?"

"Until I figure out when I can fucking trust you again or until you fuck up and I fire you." His voice was increasing in both volume and pitch. "Is that definite enough for you, Bill?"

He was glaring at Karb, the file clenched in his hands and starting to crease.

"Yes, sir."

The captain forced his hands to relax and took a deep breath.

"Okay, I want to meet with the three of you every week to see how everything is going and what cases you're working on. No promises, Bill. I need you to understand, this is it. No more chances. No more favors. I hear one whisper of you doing anything you shouldn't or that you're losing it again and you'll be gone. Got it?"

Karb replied softly, "Yes, sir."

The captain put down the file in his hand and picked up another file from his credenza. He held it up.

"I've already started drafting the paperwork for your discharge. Don't make me finish it."

Karb turned towards his captain and put his hand out to shake his hand. Schnadig looked at the proffered hand but kept his hands to himself.

"Sorry, Bill, I'm not there yet."

Karb withdrew his hand, nodded his head and then turned, a little like a whipped pup, and walked out.

༄

"Well, if it isn't Detective Bill Karb, media star and first-class asshole."

Karb sat down at his desk and looked across at Detective Carol Capobianco. She was in her early fifties, with a dark complexion and thick black hair, holding true to her southern Italian heritage. She was one of those rare women who never seem to lose their looks. He would bet she was a looker in high school and would still be catching guys' eyes when she was in her eighties. If he were more poetic, he would describe her as like a fine wine that only improves with age. Unfortunately, Karb was not poetic.

What Karb truly appreciated and respected was that she had absolutely no interest in her looks. She wore clothes that were more comfortable than fashionable. These clothes were generally ill-fitting and often stained…and she just didn't care. By the end of the day, it was more common than not for her to have food or coffee stains, or both, on her clothes.

Karb wasn't generally one to notice such things on a fellow detective but with Capobianco, he couldn't help it.

"Gee, thanks Capo. You always know just what to say to make a guy feel welcome."

"Capo, be nice," the other detective said. Debbie Pedersen was about the same age as Capobianco, but with short, blond hair and a lighter complexion. She was thin, of average height, and had the looks of a stereotypical grandmother. Her hair was always pulled back behind her ears, and she dressed very conservatively. This helped make her such an effective investigator. While Capobianco might intimidate a witness with her looks and aggressiveness, Pedersen could calm a nervous witness and quickly assume the role of a confidant. She exuded a genuine niceness that hid her fierce intellect and tenacity. Their combined talents and personalities were what made them such a successful detective team. It was more than just some sort of "good cop/bad cop" team. These two had complimentary skills and personalities that allowed them to be effective in a world that, until recently, was generally considered to be the exclusive domain of men.

He knew he was still a better detective than either of them, but that knowledge wasn't of much help in this situation.

Capobianco let out a quick laugh. "Okay, okay. So seriously, how are you doing, Bill?"

"Damned if I know but I suspect we'll all find out sooner than later."

If there was anyone Karb could work with, it would be these two.

"So, how do we do this?" Karb asked.

Capobianco stood up and placed two bankers' boxes on his desk. While Capobianco and Pedersen's desks butted up against one another, Bill's was off to the side. It was almost symbolic of the fact that he was part of the team but still separate.

"Debbie and I both have court coming up within the next two weeks. Mine is the road rage case, where a putz from Southeast shot and killed a young father for not yielding the right of way. That's set for trial. Debbie has a shopkeeper who was killed in a bungled robbery. The DA is taking that to the grand jury. We'd like you to go through both of our cases and see if we missed anything."

"Why?"

"Neither one of us wants to look like an idiot if the defense attorneys catch anything. You've been doing this longer than either of us. We figured it might serve two purposes. First, and most importantly, you're helping us avoid getting hammered on the stand. Secondly, this will ease you back into active duty."

Pedersen then added, "We don't really have any new investigations for you to work on right now. The next one that comes in, though, you'll be working on it. Is that alright with you, Bill?"

"Yeah, I guess so. It makes sense. Until then, I'll be a fresh set of eyes for you."

A begrudging smile came to Karb's face. For so long, he had been the alpha in the department and was used to being the dominant personality in his investigations. Now, and at least for the immediate future, he would have to keep his ego in check and figure out how to fit in.

"Thanks, Debbie. Thanks, Capo. I really do appreciate this. All I ask is that if you see me doing anything that concerns you, let me know before talking to the captain. Old habits die hard, and I don't want to screw up my last chance merely because I let an old habit slip through."

Pedersen spoke up first. "Absolutely, Bill. That's a more than fair request. We want you to get back in full. Don't we, Capo?"

Capobianco gave a smile that could only be described as sad and nodded her head. "Of course we do." It was clear that she had no expectation that he would be successful in doing so.

Karb reached over, opened the first box, and pulled out a file. As he started reading, Capobianco took a long look at him. He appeared tired but not yet defeated. It was clear that he was a very damaged man, and she could only hope that he could find his way out of whatever hell he was living in. They had known each other for over twenty years, and it really bothered her to see him in such obvious pain. The pain had always been there, at least as long as she had known him, but it was just more obvious now.

Pain can only be buried so long before it starts oozing out from even the bravest of facades. The emotional scars start being matched by physical manifestations that never seem to really disappear. Sometimes, like with Karb, they showed up in the lines around one's eyes and mouth. Other times it involves hunched shoulders or a slow gait that almost looks painful.

Capobianco looked over at Pedersen. Without speaking, they both knew what the other was thinking.

About an hour later, Karb put down the file he had been reviewing. He placed his pen on the yellow pad he'd been writing his notes on. There were already six pages full.

"Debbie, I've been looking at your case. Have you looked into whether the botched robbery might be gang related?"

"No, Bill. Why?"

"If I recall correctly, this is an area where the Hoover Street gang operates. I might be wrong but, well, it might be something to look into. Do you know Ed Wallace over at the Gang Enforcement Team?"

"No, I don't."

"You might want to give him a call. I can do it for you if you want. He'd be a good contact and you might want to at least talk to him."

"That sounds good. Do I mention your name?"

"Absolutely, I've known him for years and we've always had a good working relationship. Last year, when I was looking into the Patriot Boys, he was really helpful. I'm pretty sure I haven't alienated him…at least not yet."

All three of them smiled at Karb's wry humor.

"Thanks, Bill. I'll call him now."

Karb stood up and stretched his back. Looking at the other detectives, he said "I'm going to get some coffee. Want some?"

"Sure, a latte would be great. With soy milk, please," said Capobianco.

"Debbie, want anything?"

"That would be nice. Can you get me an iced coffee?"

"Got it," Karb said as he walked towards the elevators.

Chapter Six

Randy was checking his email when his telephone rang. He hated when people called his direct number. He was old school and preferred the receptionist or his assistant screen his calls. He hit the handsfree button on his phone to activate the speaker.

"Wilkerson here."

There was just a moment's delay and then he heard, "Randy, Charlene is dead!"

Randy looked up from his computer screen. "What? Jim? What the fuck happened?" His voice was loud enough that he could see his assistant, sitting just outside of his office, swivel her head.

"She fell down the stairs somehow."

"When?"

"It was sometime in the middle of the night. I found her this morning." Davies took a deep, and purposefully loud, breath. "Randy, what should I do?"

"Wow, uhm, Jim, quick, you've got to call the police."

Wilkerson saw his assistant, LaVonne, get up and stand in his doorway. He waved his hand to indicate that she should go away. She returned to her desk but could still hear everything.

"I did that already. Both the police and the EMTs came."

"Did they leave?"

"No, they are just outside, at least the cop is." Davies, standing in the kitchen, looked around the corner and saw the two EMTs still standing by the bottom of the stairs. He continued, speaking in a loud whisper, "The police officer started asking questions and I felt like I was being interrogated. He asked if he could look around and I told him no and to get out."

"Jim…"

"I told him that if he wanted to search the house, he had to talk to you first. Isn't that what I was supposed to do?"

"Jim, no. Why wouldn't you let him look around?"

"Randy, you always tell me to be courteous to the cops but don't cooperate. Isn't that what you told me?"

"Sure, but that was for something like drinking and driving, not when they want to investigate the scene of a death. You know now they're going to be suspicious and probably get a warrant."

"Is that a big deal?"

"It isn't as long as you didn't kill Char. Jim, you didn't kill Char, did you?"

"Of course not, we had both committed to working things out. Randy, this is too much. Can you come over?"

"Absolutely. I'll be there in about twenty minutes. The cop is outside, right?"

"Yeah, he said he was calling the medical examiner, and I would have to let them back in. Do I really?"

"Yeah, Jim, you do. Look, when the ME gets there, let them in and just wait for me."

"Okay…oh wait, they're knocking on the door now."

"Jim, listen to me very carefully. Let them in but don't talk to them. Do you understand?"

"Yes."

"Good, I'm leaving now. Make sure you let them in but stay out of their way."

Randy stared at his phone and could faintly hear his old friend opening the front door and then there were indistinguishable voices. He stood and as he started packing files into his briefcase, he heard, "Randy, okay, I let them in."

"Jim, how are you holding up? Are you alright?"

"I'm just shaken up. I found Charlene and, well, I've seen enough bodies to know that she was dead. I checked for a pulse and all but there was nothing. What should I do? How long will the cops be here?"

"I don't know but I'm leaving now. Remember, don't talk to the cops but also don't interfere with them. Hopefully they'll be done within an hour or so and we can then figure out what to do next."

"What do we do about Char?"

"Nothing at this point. Once the ME examines the body, you'll have to call a funeral home to pick up her body. If the ME has any concerns, he'll have her transported to the morgue."

"Why the morgue?"

"Jim, don't worry. I'll be there in about twenty or so."

Randy didn't wait for a response but disconnected the call and stood up. He almost ran into his assistant as she was coming out from around her desk. "Mr. Wilkerson, is everything alright? Was that Dr. Davies?"

"Damn it, LaVonne, I hate when you eavesdrop on my phone calls."

"I'm sorry, sir. I was just about to bring some files in and didn't want to interrupt. Is Dr. Davies alright?"

"He'll be fine," he said as he stood up and grabbed his suit jacket off the rack. "Cancel all my meetings for the rest of the morning. Also, call Bahij and tell him to call me on my cell. I need to know if there is anything I need to advise Dr. Davies of."

"Is there anything else I can do?"

"Jesus, LaVonne! How the fuck should I know? I'm not a defense attorney. I do know that I don't want you spreading any gossip. Don't say anything to anyone. Just do what I told you to."

Randy Wilkerson, a senior attorney at Thrower, Kehoe, Wilkerson & Jada, P.C., strode away and out the door. Just before he was out of earshot, he said, "I'll call you later and let you know if I'll be back today."

LaVonne Floyd picked up the phone and started making calls.

CHAPTER SEVEN

As Karb exited the elevator on the main floor of the police building, he saw a uniformed officer approach him.

"Excuse me…Detective Karb?"

Karb took a look at the young officer in front of him. It only took a few seconds to place him.

"Sprehe? Tim Sprehe, right?" Karb was honestly glad to see a friendly face. "How are you doing?"

"Uhm, pretty good, sir." Sprehe had an odd look on his face and appeared nervous. "Can we talk, sir?"

"Of course, Tim. Why don't you walk with me to the coffee shop?" For reasons he could never explain, he refused to refer to it as Starbucks. To him, it was always just a coffee shop, regardless of what name was over the door and how fancy the drinks might be.

They both turned and walked out the front door and started down the sidewalk. The temperature was moderate and there was a light drizzle of rain. Through the clouds, flashes of sunshine broke through from time to time.

Like any good Portlander, Karb eschewed umbrellas. He just buttoned up his raincoat and adjusted his hat.

"What can I do for you, Tim? You're not still manning the tape at crime scenes, are you?"

"No, sir, and I suspect I have you to thank for that. I assume you said something to my sergeant, and I appreciate that."

"No problem, all I told him was the truth."

The men walked in silence before Sprehe started, "I think I might have something but I'm not really sure."

They walked the rest of the way to the Starbucks with Sprehe explaining his interactions with Dr. Davies at the Alameda house that morning. After placing their orders, the two men took seats over by the window and waited for their drinks.

"Tim, how sure are you that it really was string and duct tape that fell out of his pocket?"

"Probably about seventy percent; it was pretty quick but the fact that I felt some sticky residue at the top of the stairs really confirmed it for me."

"How long did it take the ME to get to the house after you called him?"

"About 15 minutes, apparently dispatch had alerted them of a fatality. As soon as he got there, we knocked, and the husband let us right back in. I noticed that he had changed into a pair of khakis and a golf shirt. While the ME inspected the body, I went back up to the top of the stairs and felt for the adhesive again. It wasn't there. The baseboard was completely smooth."

"Had you told the ME about the stickiness before you went in?"

"I did, but he was focusing on the body."

"How about the EMTs? Did they see anything?"

"No, I asked them, and they saw him walk upstairs but didn't pay any attention to him once he'd stepped over the body."

Karb didn't like where this was going. Homicides are always difficult to investigate and even tougher to prosecute when the initial investigation was botched.

"Where was the husband at that time?" Karb asked.

"He had gone back into the living room and was sitting on the sofa again. As I came back down the stairs, I caught his eye and I swear he was almost smirking."

"Did you have the ME double check the baseboards at the top of the stairs?"

"Yes, sir but, like me, he found nothing. He and I did a cursory search of the upstairs, and the ME did a complete inventory of all the prescriptions we found in the master bedroom and bath."

"Do you remember what they were?"

"No, sir, but there were a lot of them."

Karb heard his name called and looked up to see Capobianco and Pedersen's drinks, as well as black coffees for him and Sprehe, sitting at the counter. The two police officers stood up and Karb placed three of the hot cups in a cardboard tray, nodded to the barista, and handed the other coffee to Sprehe. They walked out the front door and headed back to the police station.

"Okay, Tim, what happened after the initial inspection with the ME?"

"We headed down the stairs and the front door opened, and this guy came in. He identified himself as Randy Wilkerson, said he was a lawyer but was there only as a friend. I asked if the husband would be willing to come down to the station and be interviewed. The lawyer said he didn't want that. Apparently, the husband might have his reputation tarnished if he was seen going to the police station to answer questions.

"I asked if I could question the husband right then and the lawyer said yes but reminded me that his friend had just been through a traumatic incident. The funny thing to me was that the husband seemed like a totally different guy than he had been just an hour before. When I first saw him, he was frazzled and distraught. Now, he was casually dressed and seemed strangely calm. While the lawyer and I were talking, he just sat there, almost as if he was bored by all of it."

"But you did get to talk to the husband?"

"I did and he told me basically what I've already told you—he was sleeping, woke up in the morning and found his wife at the bottom of the stairs. He mentioned a couple of times that the front door was unlocked when he went down to let the EMTs in. It seemed suspicious, like he was trying to set this up as if an intruder might have come in. I asked him again about the string and tape that fell out of his pocket before, and he claimed to have no idea of what I was talking about. Detective…"

Karb interrupted, "Call me Bill. We're colleagues."

"Thank you, Detect…Bill. So…Bill, I know I haven't been doing this for long but, I swear, something is just wrong here. I really think this guy arranged to have his wife trip and fall down the stairs. I'm just not sure how we prove it."

The two men walked up the stairs to the front door of the police station. Sprehe opened it and let Karb enter first. Stopping by the elevators, Karb asked, "Tim, did you look through the kitchen and the garage to see if you could find rolls of duct tape or string?"

Sprehe dropped his head and his shoulders visibly sagged. Why hadn't he thought to do that?

Without waiting for a reply, Karb said, "Don't worry. You'll know better next time."

"Can we do it now?"

"Tim, even if we could, I'm sure we wouldn't find anything. If the husband did use tape and twine or something like that to trip his wife into falling down the stairs, he'll have gotten rid of anything like that by now."

"So, what do we do? How do we prove he killed his wife?"

"Tim, at this point, I don't know. This is certainly something we should look into. Have you written your report yet?"

"No, sir, I mean, Bill, I was planning on going up and writing it now."

"Good, take your time and be very thorough and precise with your report. Describe what you saw but acknowledge your errors. Remember, if we ever get him charged and it goes to trial, his defense attorney will go through your report with a fine-tooth comb. If it looks like you were hiding your errors, he'll crucify you. Have someone proof it for typos before you submit it. Make sure it is perfect.

"The ME took the body, right?"

"Yes, sir…" Bill held up his hand and leaned in toward the young officer. Officer Sprehe continued, "*Bill*, yes, the ME had the body transported down to the morgue."

"Tim, you did a good job, but made some serious mistakes, and you know that. You'll get better at this, I promise." Karb wasn't as confident as his voice suggested but decided that there was no need to humiliate the officer at this point. It would happen eventually and likely by his sergeant and whichever ADA might be assigned the case…if there was one.

"I'll call the ME's office and see what type of exam they're going to make. Next time, though, don't leave the house. You never want to give a suspect, or anyone else, the opportunity to clean up after him or herself."

"I know, I was just a little thrown and he seemed so emotional. I promise I won't ever do that again."

"Good, let me see what I can do. When your report is done, please send me a copy, alright?

"Of course, thanks…Bill."

They entered the elevator, each pushing the button for their respective floors.

CHAPTER EIGHT

"Joyce, thanks for meeting me." Meg stood up as Joyce McCarthy, a local, independent podcast producer walked over to her. "Let's go inside. Can I get you a drink?"

"Yes, please, a chai latte."

"I'm going to get a breakfast sandwich. Do you want one?"

"No thanks. I had a bite to eat before I came."

Both women entered the café, with Meg immediately walking over to the counter, and Joyce to a small booth in the center. Meg ordered a double espresso and a pork belly breakfast burrito, then Joyce's chai latte. As she waited for her credit card to be processed, she looked back at her companion sitting at the booth and looking out the open windows. The café had three garage-style doors, one in the front and two to the side. All of them were opened completely to let the unseasonably warm air in.

Joyce was in her mid- to late-30s, with streaks of prematurely gray hair. She was short, with an athletic physique. She carried a wooden cane, but Meg couldn't determine if this was for a utilitarian purpose or just aesthetics. She walked back and sat across from Joyce.

"Meg, how did you find this place?"

"Either/Or is one of my favorite little cafés. A friend told me about it before I left for New York. The coffee is good, but the food is absolutely decadent, plus they have a full bar. You sure you don't want something to eat?"

"No, I'm good. I've got another meeting at 1:00, so we need to be quick."

"Okay, I'll cut to the chase. I want you to work on my podcast."

"Are you back?"

"Yeah, I miss this little shithole of a city." Meg smiled and Joyce smiled back.

"Are you looking for a fulltime or parttime producer?"

"Fulltime."

"Alright, but Meg, you never really used a fulltime producer before. Your podcast was great. Why change?"

"Joyce, I've come to realize how important this podcast is to me. I want to take it to the next level, to be the best it can be, and I don't think I can do that on my own."

"What are you looking for from me?"

"I'll still do all the leg work and the basic writing, but I just want some help with reviewing the script, as well as the recording and editing. I'm proud of the podcast but think it could be more professional and I know your work."

"Meg, I'm honored, of course, but I'm pretty busy these days. Have you talked with anyone else?"

"Joyce, you're it. I know your talents and I know your style. I think we'd be good together."

Joyce was flattered to be her first and only choice, although a flicker of doubt made Joyce wonder whether Meg was being completely truthful.

Joyce had been producing podcasts for the past eight years and seen more than her share fail. The failures, however, were generally because the creators failed to realize the amount of work involved or lost their enthusiasm, or both. She knew Meg wasn't like them. Meg had built her podcast into a local success and garnered enough attention to get a position on national television. She had to wonder what the story was behind Meg leaving *20/20* and whether it was her choice or theirs.

That, however, would be a discussion for another day.

"When you say you want to make it more professional, what do you mean?"

Just then, the women heard Meg's name called by the barista. Meg quickly walked over and picked up the drinks and her breakfast burrito. Upon returning, she placed Joyce's latte in front of her and sat down. She immediately unwrapped her burrito and took a large bite. She chewed slowly as she worked to formulate just the right answer to Joyce's question.

She picked up her napkin, wiped her mouth, and then took a sip of her espresso. Finally finished, she took a breath and looked at Joyce.

"I want this to be more than just a local podcast. I'm thinking that we could handle stories other than just in Portland. Seattle is close enough that I could keep most of the same sponsors and slowly expand our audience. If that works, and we can find some more talent, maybe even build this into a brand with other investigators in other cities. True crime podcasts are really hot right now and I want to take advantage of the interest."

"Meg, I don't know…"

"Joyce, you know I've got a quality podcast. With your help, we can make it so much better. I really need you."

Joyce took a sip of her latte and looked at Meg. She hadn't seen her in more than a year and she looked almost ragged. Meg had never been a fashion maven, but she was always attractive. Now her hair was somewhat bedraggled, and she seemed too thin. Joyce had to wonder whether Meg might have problems handling the rigors of growing a national podcast.

"Meg, I agree that you've got a quality podcast, but I'm not really interested in just being a hired gun for you."

"What do you mean?"

"If we do this, and that's a big 'if', I want to be partners with you. I want a say in what stories you do and how they are presented. If the possibility arises to take this to the next level, I want to be involved in those decisions."

Meg looked at Joyce. She was not entirely happy with the prospect of sharing her show.

"So, you want an equity stake?"

"I do. I'm at the point in my life when I want to be more than just a freelance producer. I want to be part of building something I can claim some ownership in. Is that going to be a problem?"

Meg took another bite of her burrito. She knew that she needed Joyce but had left the network gig because of the lack of control. The prospect of giving up even a little control of her podcast was concerning.

"I don't know. It's not something I was really thinking about."

"Meg, I don't want to push you to do something you don't want to do. Let's agree to think a bit more on this and talk more in a couple of days. What stories are you working on now?"

Meg finished the burrito and washed it down with a large sip of her espresso.

"Yeah, that's a problem. There's nothing that has rung the bell for me. I'm still looking for the right story. The fact that I don't have one yet gives us a little time to get set up and figure out how to work with one another."

"Okay, but we can't take too long. I'm working on a number of podcasts and if we agree to work together…as partners, I'm going to have to drop at least a couple of the others. The nice thing is that I've got contacts with various sponsors who know of my reputation and might be interested in our podcast."

Joyce had struck a chord with Meg. She had never really enjoyed selling herself to sponsors, although she had done it well enough to generate a reasonable income. The thought of having Joyce take over the marketing part of the business was very appealing.

"Okay, let's plan on meeting at my apartment and talk this through. I'll need some time to think about your proposal. Are you available on Friday night?"

"It's not a proposal, Meg," Joyce interrupted her. "It is an idea, one that we both need to really flesh out before I can commit to you."

Meg nodded. "You're right and that's fair. Let's both come up with some bullet points and see if we can figure it out."

"That's a great idea. I'll probably talk to my brother, he's a lawyer over at Sussman Shank, and see if he might have some ideas as to issues for us to work through. One last question."

"Shoot," Meg responded.

"How do you stay so thin eating crap like that?"

Meg smiled and simply said, "Good genes, I guess."

With a shake of her head, Joyce took a final sip of her latte and they both stood up.

"Meg, it's been nice to see you again and thanks for the coffee. Friday about 7:00?"

"Perfect."

"Are you still in the same place?"

"Yeah, I sublet while in New York but I'm back in it."

"Should I bring some Thai?"

"That would be perfect. I'll see you then."

They gave each other a brief hug and walked out the door of the Either/Or Cafe. Meg turned left on North Williams Street and Joyce turned right. The sun was covered by clouds and Meg felt a sudden chill in the air. Looking back, she noticed Joyce walking with a slight limp in her gait.

Meg felt the telephone in her pocket vibrate. She reached in and put it to her ear.

"Hello?"

"Is this Meg Nguyen?"

"Yes, who's this?" Meg recognized it as a man's voice, but it was muffled.

"The podcaster?"

"Yes."

"Charlene Price Davies. Check it out."

"Who? What are…" The line clicked dead.

CHAPTER NINE

Karb turned the corner and saw Capobianco and Pedersen at their desks. Neither noticed him until he set their drinks down.

Pedersen looked up first. "Thanks, Bill."

Capobianco followed, "Yeah, thanks Bill, but did you ever consider going to a local Starbucks? You've been gone for almost an hour."

Karb gave a wan smile in response. He appreciated Capobianco's ribbing and that it was standard fare amongst detectives, but that had never been Karb's style. For just a moment, he wondered if that was something he should discuss with Dr. Malone. As quickly as the thought came to him, it left.

"Okay, I may have something."

Both Capobianco and Pedersen looked at him.

"What have you got?" Pedersen asked.

Over the next thirty minutes, Karb walked them through everything that Officer Sprehe had told him. They discussed Sprehe exiting the house while the ME was called and his not properly securing the scene. Regrettably, it was something that they'd have to deal with.

The two women perked up at the mention of the attorney who had come to the home as a friend of the husband's.

"What did you say the attorney's name was?" Pedersen asked.

"Wilkerson, I think," Karb responded.

Capobianco interjected, "Randy Wilkerson?"

"Yeah, I guess. You heard of him?"

Capobianco and Pedersen looked at each other and started laughing broadly as they slowly turned back to Karb.

"Really? You've never heard of Randy Wilkerson? Okay, I guess I can understand why. You're a guy."

"What the hell are you talking about?"

"Bill," Pedersen said, "Randy Wilkerson is known as the Silver Fox. For decades now, he's been Portland's most eligible bachelor. He's gorgeous and charming and rich. I promise, you can ask any woman over thirty and she'll know of him."

"So other than the fact that he's good-looking, what's the big deal?"

"Bill, he's not just good-looking. Saying that is like saying Brad Pitt is *just* good-looking."

"Who's Brad Pitt?"

The two detectives again laughed out loud, loud enough to cause everyone else in the detective division to look over at them.

"All right, Bill, let's just say that Randy Wilkerson is well-known amongst those who pay attention to such things. If for no other reason than him, this case now has our attention. The prospect of Debbie and I getting to meet the Silver Fox is very appealing."

"Fine, whatever, you can talk to him, but we need to figure out how to handle this investigation."

Capobianco said, "Your young friend hasn't given us much to work with. The mysterious ball of string and duct tape and the missing tape residue won't get us anywhere with the DA's office. Hell, I'm not sure we'll even be able to convince the captain that this is worth investigating."

Karb noticed that Capobianco had spilled a little of her coffee on her shirt. She absently wiped it with her hand and then wiped her wet hand on her pants.

Karb responded, "I get that. I'm hoping that the ME's report will give us something to hang our hats on."

"Agreed," said Pedersen.

"If, and I know it's a big if," Karb continued, "the ME's report gives us something, I'd like to come up with a strategy on how to attack this case. I was thinking that we could talk to the wife's friends, as well as the neighbors."

"Slow down, Bill," Capobianco said, "we can't do any of that without some reasonable basis for suspicion of foul play, especially as we're talking about the Alameda neighborhood and Portland's upper crust." She could sense Bill's excitement. When he suspected criminal wrongdoing, he was like a dog with a bone. He just couldn't give it up.

Both Capobianco and Pedersen noticed him fidgeting in his chair. He wanted to pursue this right away.

Pedersen added, "Bill, I've got an idea you won't like."

Karb looked at her.

"We can't take this to the captain yet. I'll call the ME's office and first see if they'd be willing to do a full forensic autopsy on the vic rather than just the standard clinical."

"I can do that," Karb said.

"Bill, no you can't," Pedersen said. "I don't know how you pissed them off down there but my contacts there made it clear that you are unwelcome in that department. It seemed to be coming from Maureen Huey, but I couldn't get any other details. Care to let us in on what you did to piss her off?"

Karb just shrugged and muttered, "No."

"Okay, then I'll call down there. It's still going to take a week or so and there's not much we can do until then, at least not officially."

"What do you mean by 'officially'?"

Pedersen looked at him. "Bill, I'm going to talk to Meg."

Bill almost jumped out of his chair. "NO!"

The two detectives waited for him to regain his composure.

"Don't get her involved. I can start looking into this in my off time."

"No, Bill, you can't." Capobianco leaned forward and lowered her voice. "You're on a very short leash and if the captain finds out you've initiated an investigation without running it by him first, especially when we're dealing with some very wealthy and well-connected people, you'll be gone within a week."

Karb stared at her wordlessly.

"You know I'm right."

Still, he didn't respond.

Pedersen broke the silence. "Bill, we're going to talk to Meg and give her only the minimum of information. We won't mention the tape or the string. We'll only mention that this is an incident that she might find of interest. I promise that we'll be very careful."

Just then, Capobianco's telephone rang. She picked up her cellphone, smiled, and answered it on speakerphone. "Detective Capobianco here…hello Meg. We were just talking about you."

The three detectives looked at one another. The scowl on Karb's face was prominent.

"Hey, Capo, quick question. Have you heard anything about the death of a woman named Charlene Davies?"

The smile immediately drained from Capobianco's face. Both Pedersen and Karb noticed.

"Meg, look, I'm in the middle of something right now. Can I get back to you later today?"

"Sure, I'm just fishing and heard something."

"Yeah, okay. I'll get back to you."

Capobianco hung up the phone and looked at the other two.

Karb spoke first, "How the fuck did she hear about this?"

"Bill, you know it wasn't us. You just told us. We wouldn't have had the opportunity to call her."

"Fuck!" Capobianco said under her breath, but just loud enough to be heard by her companions.

Pedersen responded, "Okay, we can't play this as slowly as we thought. If Meg finds something, we've got to get ahead of it or else we'll look like idiots."

Karb rubbed his eyes with both hands, attempting to clear his thoughts, as well as to give himself a moment to think.

"We've got to talk to the captain. I agreed with you before about the need to slow play this but…"

"Bill," Capobianco interrupted him. "Do you think it was your uniform buddy, the one who fucked up the initial investigation? Might he have talked to Meg?"

Karb took a moment to think about this before responding, "No, it wasn't him. Tim's a good kid and was really embarrassed by his screwups. The last thing he'd do would be to talk to someone like Meg. This had to have come from someone else, but who?"

Both of the female detectives looked at him, slowly shaking their heads.

"I don't want to wait for Sprehe's report. We need to talk to the captain today. Are you both available this afternoon?"

"I'm not," Pedersen responded. "My bungled robbery perp is being transported to Clackamas County for an arraignment on a case out there. I'm going with him. I talked with your buddy, Ed Wallace, and he suggested I talk to the perp on the ride. We'll see if we can't get him to talk about the Hoover Street gang and whether he might be willing to flip and trade info for a possible sentence reduction. With cases both here and Clackamas County, Ed thought it might be worth a shot. You two can go, though. It's not like I've got any info that you don't."

"Alright, good luck with the gangbanger. I'll call the captain and see," he said, looking at Capobianco, "if he can fit us in this afternoon. Before we do that, can you call the ME and see if they'll do a full autopsy?"

"I'll call now."

Karb rolled his chair back to his desk and started to type on his computer. Capobianco picked up her telephone and started dialing the ME's office whilst Pedersen started studying her file. She needed to get up to speed on the Hoover Street gang quickly.

CHAPTER TEN

Wilkerson was typing on his laptop when he heard a commotion and his door was flung open.

"Uncle Randy, what happened?"

Wilkerson swiftly stood up and strode over to the young woman who had just entered. Kelly Price was almost nineteen now. She was thin and wearing ragged jeans and an old Rolling Stones' t-shirt. Her hair was cut in an asymmetrical style, and he noticed a small ring in her nose.

"Oh, Peanut, I'm so sorry."

She started sobbing in his arms. Wilkerson looked up and saw his assistant staring at them. He motioned with his head for her to get back to work.

"What happened? You mentioned an accident, and then I saw on the news that she fell down the stairs. Is she really dead?"

"Kelly, your mom must have tripped in the middle of the night. Jim found her in the morning."

Wilkerson could feel the girl's body stiffen up at the mention of her stepfather.

"Come here, sit down. Can I get you something to drink?"

"Can I have some tea, please?"

The girl's voice was weak, presumably from both exhaustion and grief. Looking up at his assistant who was still standing in the doorway, Wilkerson said, "LaVonne, get a cup of tea for Kelly and some coffee for me."

Mrs. Floyd immediately walked away to get the drinks.

Wilkerson sat in the client chair beside Kelly and reached for her hand.

"You know your mom loved you, right? She really did."

"Uncle R, we hadn't talked in over a month. I was just so…I guess I was just still so angry with her about…him."

"Kelly, the fact that your mom loved your stepfather doesn't mean she loved you any less."

The girl looked up, tears welling up in her eyes. "I know that in my head, but my heart tells me that she chose him and rejected me. I know that sounds crazy but that's just the way I feel. Oh, I'm such an asshole!"

"Kelly, you're not an asshole. It is common for mothers and daughters to have some tension, especially in a situation like yours with a stepfather. She loved you and it was only a matter of time before the two of you would have reconnected completely again."

"But that's the problem, Uncle R. That's never going to happen now. In our last conversation, I hung up on her."

Leaning in and putting her hands to his lips, he kissed them and said, "Kelly, I know how tough this is but it's going to be alright. I promise. It's just going to take some time."

Just then Mrs. Floyd came back and placed the tea and coffee on the desk. Kelly looked up at the legal assistant and thanked her.

Mrs. Floyd retreated to her desk but left the door open.

"What happens next?"

"Well, we're working on having a celebration of life for your mom at the MAC Club."

"God, I hate that term—*celebration of life*. Why can't we just say that it's a wake or a commemoration of her life or some shit like that. No one is going to be celebrating…well, except for *him*."

"Kelly, don't talk like that. For all his faults, Jim loved your mom. He certainly wasn't your dad, but he loved your mom."

Wilkerson reached into his back pocket and pulled out a handkerchief, handing it to her. She wiped her eyes and then blew her nose loudly. Handing the handkerchief back to Wilkerson, she shyly said, "sorry."

"Uncle R, I don't want to be crass, but what happens to the trust now? Do I become the trustee?"

Wilkerson slowly shook his head and responded, "It's not quite that simple. It's going to take a while to figure out exactly what happens next. Your dad wanted me to run the trust after he passed so I'll stay in that role. Your stepdad is a beneficiary also and we need to figure out how to divvy up the assets. In the meantime, I'm going to increase your monthly stipend until we can figure things out. You're going to inherit a good amount of money when you turn thirty and I want you to meet with a financial advisor now to start planning. Your dad specifically told me that when you inherited your share of the trust, he wanted you to work with a good financial advisor who could help you, so you should start interviewing potential advisors to find a good fit."

"Could that be you?"

Wilkerson gave a sad smile and said, "Maybe, Kelly, maybe."

He leaned back and looked at the young girl sitting beside him. "You know, your parents were always so proud of you. I'm sure that wherever they are now, they still are."

They talked for a few more minutes and then Wilkerson called out to his assistant. "LaVonne, make a reservation for a room at The Nines for Ms. Price. Give them my credit card."

Looking back at Kelly, he continued, "Stay there for the next week or so. Once we have a better idea of what the MAC can do, we'll talk. If you want to speak at the…event, just let me know. If you don't, that will be fine too."

"Thanks, Uncle R."

The two of them stood up and embraced again. Wilkerson led her to the door, kissed her on the cheek and then steered her towards his assistant before walking back into his office, closing the door behind him.

$$\text{\small ❧}$$

Chapter Eleven

"The captain said he can meet with us at 3:00 pm today. He didn't seem happy to hear from me."

"Well, Bill, can you blame him? You've only been back for two days and you're already bringing a problem to him," Capobianco said. She knew that Karb was on thin ice with the captain and wasn't sure how he would respond to their talk.

"How about if you let me take the lead? You can correct me if I misstate anything that the uniform told you and fill in any holes."

Karb looked at her, understanding what she was doing.

"Thanks," he said.

"We don't need to tell him everything, at least not at this point. I want to let him know the basics, and that the ME is doing the full forensic before mentioning that Meg called us."

Karb squeezed his eyes shut and started to rub his temples. Meg Nguyen always seemed to make his life more difficult. He could begrudgingly admit that she had some investigative skills but that didn't make her any less problematic.

"Yeah, that makes sense." Karb looked at his watch. It was already 1:45 pm. "I'll continue working the news and social media to see what I can find out about Charlene Davies and her husband.

"Let's plan on talking about 2:30, so we can bring each other up to date on anything additional that we've found and finalize how to present it to the captain."

"Sure, Bill, that'll be great."

The two detectives turned away from one another and got to work.

Shortly before 2:30 pm, Karb stood up and said, "Capo, let's go down to the interrogation rooms and talk. I've got some good info for you."

The two of them walked down the hall to the first open interrogation room. While this wasn't the main purpose of these rooms, detectives found them convenient to have conversations in private and be able to speak freely. Until they brought this to the captain, they didn't want the rumor mill that runs deep throughout the police station to get into gear.

Capobianco sat down first and placed a yellow legal pad in front of her on the table, pen in hand ready to write notes.

Karb began, "Well, she, more than he, was heavily involved in the city's social scene. I found numerous references to her attending this fundraiser or that, as well as galas…I didn't even know galas were still a thing."

"Yes, Bill, they are, but not for the likes of you or me."

"That figures. Anyway, she was on the Board of Directors of the Opera and the Art Museum. She also seemed to be heavily involved with Janus Youth Programs, which is a non-profit that helps homeless kids."

"What about her background? Is she from here?"

Karb flipped his pad of paper to another page. "Yeah, born and bred in Portland. She went to Catlin Gable and then Reed College. She was married to a guy named Ken Price. He was one of the early execs at Nike and apparently did well with stock options."

"What happened to him?"

"He went in for a bypass procedure and bled out on the table. They had one kid—a daughter, Kelly. I couldn't find much on her yet. Anyways, they were left pretty well off. There's no mortgage on the house on Alameda, and she also owns a place down in Gearhart and a condo in Sunriver."

"How did she come to marry Dr. Davies?"

"I don't have anything on that yet. They'd been married for about four years, but I saw no mention of him in the news and he has no presence on social media.

"In going through her friends and photos, I identified a couple of people we might be able to talk to. One is a gal named Michelle Polidori. From her Facebook posts, it appears that she and Charlene have been friends since high school. From the tone of them, she's more than a bit melodramatic. It's almost like she sees herself as much of a victim of Charlene's death as Charlene is."

"Oh, crap," Capobianco responded, "we call those people grief chasers. Well, at least we'll know how to play her. If we recognize the enormity of her loss, she should open up…they usually do."

"Yeah, that sounds about right. Do you have anything for me?"

"I convinced the ME to do the full forensic. They asked if you were working the case and I lied and said no. That'll piss them off when they find out, but I'll deal with that when I have to."

A small smile came to Karb's lips. One of the things he liked about Capobianco was that, as the saying goes, she had balls. While Pedersen charmed people with her grandmotherly charm, Capobianco could be like a bull in a China shop who never completely breaks anything. People were quick to forgive her and Karb wondered if he would ever be able to reestablish his reputation and have others treat him like that. It was unlikely, he knew, so not something he could worry about.

"Anything else?"

"Yup, the lawyer, Randy Wilkerson? Apparently, he and Dr. Davies go back all the way to college. He was also friends with Charlene and her first husband. Rumor is that he set up a family trust for them before the husband died and that he took over as trustee five plus years ago after the husband died. Given the likely size of the trust, he could be pocketing some serious cash for that."

"So, what are you going to tell the captain?" Karb asked.

"I'm going to start with what your officer Sprehe said but won't dwell on the string and tape debacle. I'll just tell him that something didn't feel right so we're looking into it. I'll then apologize for bringing such a weak case to him but then tell him about Meg's call."

Karb shook his head, not knowing if Capobianco really understood how much the reference to Meg Nguyen would fire the captain up. Karb might not like Meg, but the captain detested her. He saw her as a constant irritation that did nothing but make his department look like the Keystone Kops. In the captain's mind, she always seemed to point out the errors the police made, rather than acknowledging their successes.

For a moment, Karb wondered if he should give a heads up to Sprehe. When the captain found out how badly Sprehe had screwed up, he was going to go ballistic. Sprehe wouldn't lose his job, but he might be back to working the tape lines at crime scenes again. Yeah, Karb decided, he'd give Sprehe a heads up the next morning.

Capobianco looked at her watch and stood up. "It's showtime. Remember, Bill, only speak if I totally misstate something or if the captain asks. Let me take the lead on this and if heat comes down, it'll be on me. Agreed?"

"Agreed," Karb responded. "And thanks. I appreciate what you're doing."

Capobianco nodded, gathered up her notes and walked out of the room. As they left, they saw a number of people racing ahead of them. Everyone was talking but neither Karb nor Capobianco could make out what they were saying.

Karb grabbed a detective nearby. "What's going on?"

"Didn't you hear? A car bomb went off in Oregon City. Apparently, Debbie was in the car."

Chapter Twelve

Welcome to Season Four of Murder in Bridge City, *my podcast for those interested in exploring the violent and ugly underbelly of our fair city of Portland, Oregon. I am your host, Meg Nguyen, and this is Episode One. I hope all of you are well and avoiding the dark side of our city of roses.*

For our new listeners, I want to give you a little background on me. I was in law enforcement for five years in Southern Oregon before moving up to Portland and starting this podcast delving into crime in and around the metropolitan area. Most recently, I took a break and hosted a 20/20 investigation of the gruesome murder of a child in Seattle.

If you saw the episode on your local ABC affiliate, I hope you enjoyed it. While it was an honor and a great experience to work on a program like 20/20, I decided to return to Portland and this podcast. I'm pleased to announce that I'm now working with Portland's top podcast producer Joyce McCarthy. I hope that together, we can keep you both informed and entertained.

What makes this podcast different from most other true crime podcasts is that much of what we do is in real time, or at least as close to real time as we can get. We don't do a historical account after a trial and conviction. There are plenty of very fine podcasts that adopt that approach. We just do things a little differently. We identify local suspicious deaths immediately after they occur, track the investigations all the way through, and pursue our own leads. We conduct our own independent investigations of witnesses, suspects, and alibis—along with the police—and report to you when a case finally goes to trial.

When we find out something new about a case, we let you know right away. Like the victims and the victims' families and friends, you will share in the frustration in the slow, and seemingly interminable, progress of criminal investigations. Some of these police investigations will go pretty much dormant in the period between arrest and trial but we won't. We'll continue our investigation and give you as much information about the victims and suspects as possible.

Over the years, I've been able to develop sources within the various law enforcement agencies throughout the area, which gives me a unique insight and perspective into ongoing criminal investigations. I have also been fortunate to develop relationships with various prosecuting and defense attorneys around Portland.

Yes, you might say I have friends in high places, as well as some in low places. I protect my contacts' anonymity and much of the information they provide to me, which then allows me to get more information from them and, ultimately, to you. Sometimes I have to withhold information from you, the listeners. I don't like doing that, but it can be necessary as I don't want to interfere with the potential prosecution of a murderer. At the end of the day, we always want the bad guys brought to justice. Sometimes that happens and sometimes it doesn't.

In this season, we're looking at three incidents, one a clear case of murder most vile, the second a suspicious death of a Portland socialite, and the other an unsettling death of a young woman who was a student at Lewis & Clark University. I'll address the latter two in a moment, but I first want to talk about the murder as it is personal to me.

As you've surely heard by now, just last week, a car bomb detonated in Oregon City that killed a longtime Portland detective and a murder suspect, as well as seriously injuring another Portland homicide detective who is a very close friend of mine–Debra Jane Pedersen.

Debbie is one of the finest detectives in the Portland Police Department and an even better person. We've been close friends for over five years. She is the mother of two great kids, a boy and a girl, and the grandmother to two. Before I go forward, while she has been very supportive of this podcast, I just want to say that she has never been one of my sources on any investigation. We are friends and I would never jeopardize that friendship by asking her for information regarding an ongoing police investigation.

Debbie and fellow detective, Edward Wallace, were to transport a suspect from the Portland city jail to the courthouse in Oregon City for an arraignment in Clackamas County. The suspect was a guy named Carlos Arriaza, who was currently in jail pending trial for murder. He was apparently also a suspect in a string of armed robberies around Oregon City and was to be arraigned down there. I've got a number of questions, principally as to why Debbie was involved in the transport of Arriaza down to Clackamas County.

I know she was the lead detective on his murder charge, but it is unclear why she was involved in his transport on unrelated crimes. Ordinarily Portland detectives wouldn't be involved in investigations in another county.

In any event and as I understand it, Detective Wallace was behind the wheel and Debbie was placing the suspect in the backseat. As she closed the door, the car exploded. Detective Wallace and Arriaza were killed instantly. Debbie was thrown over twenty feet through the air and suffered serious injuries. In addition to a concussion, she had her left leg amputated below the knee and lost her left eye. She remains in the ICU, although her condition has most recently been reported as stable.

I've been able to visit with her once and can't fully explain how remarkable this woman is. She remains upbeat despite her injuries.

Look, I'm not a religious person but if you are, you may want to say a prayer for this special woman, as well as for the widow and children of detective Edward Wallace.

Now, since this was a bomb, the feds have gotten involved, and I've learned that investigators with the FBI and the Bureau of Alcohol, Tobacco, and Firearms are working this investigation very hard. They are examining each and every piece of the destroyed vehicle, as well as bomb fragments. My sources tell me that it was a relatively sophisticated bomb and that it was remotely detonated.

Given my knowledge of these particular federal investigators, I am confident that they will have some news for us shortly. As soon as I hear anything, I will let you know.

Let's take a quick break to hear from one of our new sponsors. When we return, I'll talk about another possible murder we're going to be looking into.

 captions

Welcome back. As I mentioned before, we've got three separate deaths, all actual or potential murders, that we're following. One is the car bomb attack on the Portland Police Department which killed veteran detective Edward Wallace, a homicide suspect, and seriously injured another police detective, Debbie Pedersen.

The second matter we are exploring is the suspicious death of Portland socialite Charlene Price Davies.   Some of you may have heard of her; she grew up here in Portland as Charlene Cutler. If that last name sounds familiar, it's because her family was once one of the largest commercial real estate owners in the Northwest. She really has, or should I say had, an impressive pedigree.

Char, as she was most commonly known, attended Portland's Catlin Gable School from preschool through high school and then Vassar College back in Poughkeepsie, New York. It was about that time that Char's father was caught up in a number of scandals, sentenced to seven years in prison for tax fraud, and lost the family fortune.

After graduation, she returned to Portland and quickly met and married Ken Price, Nike's first general counsel. He was one of Nike's first one hundred employees and did very well with stock options.

They had what was, by all accounts, a great marriage and had one daughter, Kelly Price.

Unfortunately, about six years ago, Ken Price passed away during open-heart surgery. A couple of years later, Char married a local anesthesiologist, James Davies. There was some friction between the daughter Kelly and Dr. Davies, which isn't uncommon between a stepdaughter and a stepfather.

Kelly moved to Seattle and Char and Dr. Davies settled into a lovely mansion in Portland's Alameda neighborhood with an expansive view of downtown Portland.

A week ago, a 911 call was placed by Dr. Davies when he found his wife at the bottom of the stairs…dead.

Now this might have just been a tragic accident, but given the people involved, it is certainly worth looking into and that is exactly what we are going to do. To the best of my knowledge, the police are not treating this as anything other than a simple slip and fall death and it may turn out to be exactly that. Or…it could turn out to be something more deserving of our attention. I have reason to believe it may be the latter but can't disclose why just yet.

Dr. Davies has a friend who is also one of Portland's leading estate planning and tax attorneys, Randy Wilkerson. You'll love what I'll tell you about him. He could be a whole episode just by himself.

The third death is that of Erin McCann, a junior at Lewis & Clark University. Erin was found dead in the basement of the Alpha Beta Delta fraternity house. We don't know much yet as to the cause of death. We've been told that the ME's office hasn't completed the autopsy yet, but I've heard some rumors. Out of respect for her family, I won't push those rumors until I can confirm them.

In any event, this report, at least so far, has given you a very basic overview of the people whose lives we will be looking into. I'll have more for you next week.

≪≫

Chapter Thirteen

"So, Bill, how are you doing today?"

"Fine," he responded tersely.

Dr. Malone let out an audible sigh of frustration. "We don't really have the time to spend each session getting you to open up. They are only fifty-minute long, and I can't waste ten or fifteen minutes each time letting you warm up and let down your guard. So, I'm going to give it another shot. Bill, how are you doing today?"

Karb took a moment to remember that Dr. Malone wasn't the enemy. She had given him the opportunity to return to active duty and he should be grateful. That, unfortunately, wasn't a sentiment that came easily.

"Okay, I guess. I enjoy working on cases again, even if I don't have my usual freedom, but something happened this last week that…well, it shook me a bit."

"Would you like to talk about it?"

"No."

This time, Dr. Malone allowed herself a small smile as she chided herself for asking such a pointless question. Of course, Bill Karb wouldn't want to talk about it. That's why he had been ordered to undergo therapy so that he could find a way to start talking, despite his natural reticence.

"I assume you're thinking about Debbie Pedersen?"

Karb just nodded and looked over Dr. Malone's shoulder at a new abstract painting on the wall behind her. It was a horse running at full gallop, but it only appeared to have three legs. He wondered if this had some special meaning.

"You were close to Debbie, weren't you?"

Karb suddenly shifted his focus back to Dr. Malone. "I still am," he said, perhaps a bit too defensively.

"Of course, Bill, I wasn't trying to suggest or imply anything. How's Debbie doing? I've heard she's out of the ICU. Have you seen her yet?"

'Yeah, Capo and I went up to the hospital on Monday. She was pretty upbeat but still looked like crap. I don't envy her having to go through rehab. That's going to be tough."

"Have you heard anything about who did it?"

Karb shook his head. "I can't talk about that."

Dr. Malone sat up straight and corrected him. "Yes, Bill, you *can*. Remember these sessions are completely confidential. With very, very few exceptions, you and I can talk about anything. Given that you were working with Detective Pedersen at the time of the incident, and that you've known her for over twenty years, it is important for us to talk about her and how she was injured."

She stared at him, while he continued to stare behind her. She could sense him working through the logistics of what he felt comfortable talking about and what he didn't. He was sharp enough to know that he would eventually have to talk about some things even if he wasn't comfortable doing so. That, however, was somewhere down the line. The bombing would be an acceptable topic for him to talk about.

"Well, we're not doing the investigation. With the use of an explosive device and the fact that this might have been terrorist-related, the feds have taken over the case. They don't tell us much, but we hear things."

"What have you heard?"

"It sounds like they have found a fingerprint on a fragment of the bomb casing. If they can match it to anyone in the federal database, they'll likely have the guy."

Dr. Malone nodded her head but decided to switch topics slightly. "Bill, with Detective Pedersen out of the office, what's happening with her cases?"

"Well, Doc, she was prepping for a trial of the gangbanger who got blown up. That case is now gone, obviously. She's got a couple of smaller matters that are still early on and those are being shifted over to other teams."

"The captain hasn't assigned them to you?"

Karb moved his shoulders around, as if trying to fight off the frustration that was tightening up his muscles. He then simply said, "No."

Again, she decided to switch topics. Her goal was to get Bill to feel comfortable talking about all aspects of his life and it was important, at least as this stage, not to focus to heavily on any one area.

"As you still going to the gym?"

"Yeah, I'm not sparring much lately but still work out on the speed bag and the heavy bag. I'm trying to go there after work to let the sweat clear my mind. It exhausts me and helps me fall asleep quickly when I get home."

"Is there a reason you're not sparring much?"

Karb looked at her a bit quizzically, wondering if she was trying to read into something that just wasn't there.

"No, why does that matter?"

"Well, Bill, it doesn't take much to draw a conclusion that sparring with younger and much better fighters might be a way for you to punish yourself…maybe, or maybe not. What do you think?"

"Doc, I think you're reading far too much into that. Sometimes I spar and sometimes I don't. There's really no rhyme or reason. Often, I just do it if Coach wants me to work with one of his kids. It's really not a big deal."

Dr. Malone looked down at her pad of paper and started writing. This was an issue that she'd want to bring up in the future when Bill opened up a bit more. She was convinced that his decision whether or not to spar wasn't random at all. It was likely a coping mechanism for him when his emotions ran too high. Getting the crap beat out of him might be a pressure release. The fact that he was always overmatched suggests that he might need to assuage his guilt more than just work off his anger.

"Do you ever go out for a beer or anything with your friend from the gym? Coach, maybe?"

"Not really, we don't have the kind of friendship. He's a good guy, but we leave our friendship at the gym."

"Why is that?"

"I don't know, it just is."

"So, if you want to go out with someone and grab a beer, who would that be?" Dr. Malone knew the answer but needed to have Bill say it.

Karb took a moment before simply saying, "I don't know."

"Bill, one of our goals in this process is to help you develop your life so that it's more than merely work and the gym. I know you used to spend time with Mike Kelley and his family, but they're gone now. It is important that you develop new friends."

"Why?"

"Why is it important to make new friends?" She wasn't ready for that question.

"Yeah, why? Why can't I just continue as I'm doing? I'm not hurting anyone and I'm doing my job."

"Bill, one of the reasons you are here is because you don't have a healthy outlet for the stresses you experience, including, but not limited to, the difficulties of your job. Investigating homicides, you see the worst of people and what they can do. You started lashing out at co-workers. Your captain, at least in his opinion, believed that you had become erratic and possibly a danger to yourself.

"Your own personal experiences have only added to those stresses. If you don't have a healthy outlet for all of that, you… well, you'll continue to have the problems you've been experiencing over the past couple of years, only without a career anymore."

Karb looked at her and opened his mouth to start to speak. Dr. Malone held up her hand and continued, "So, no, going to the gym to box isn't enough. You need people in your life. People you can talk to. People you can laugh with. People you can rely upon. Bill, these types of people are called friends, and you need some."

Karb didn't respond, but just started looking, again, at the abstract horse painting behind Dr. Malone.

She looked at him and saw that he was trying to distract himself from the current line of discussions. "Bill, I've got some homework for you."

Karb let out a guttural laugh, "Homework? Isn't that a bit juvenile?"

"Not in the least. Look, I've got to go out of town next week, so we won't talk again until the week after. At some point over the next two weeks, I want you to go out and have lunch or dinner with someone. I don't care if it's Coach or one of your co-workers or anyone else. I want you to invite someone out for a meal. Next time we meet, we're going to talk about how it went."

"What if I don't?"

"Bill, I'm not trying to punish you with this project. As I explained before, part of a healthy life is having friends. Right now, you don't have any. You're going to do this, not because you fear me telling the captain that you aren't cooperating, but because you know this is something you need."

Karb recognized the veiled threat in her words, but also begrudgingly agreed with her.

"Yeah, okay. I'll see what I can do."

"Good, Bill. We're slowly making some progress. It will get better. Just be patient. As you develop other aspects of your life, you may even find work becoming easier."

"Doc, I'm not really looking for easier."

"Yes, I know, but I suspect your captain is, so let's do this my way, alright?"

"Sure, Doc. I'll see you in a couple of weeks."

Both Karb and Dr. Malone stood, and she extended her hand. Karb shook it with a wan smile, turned and left.

Dr, Malone sat back down at her desk and picked up her Dictaphone.

☙

CHAPTER FOURTEEN

Karb sat at his desk, working on Capobianco's road rage file. Off to the side were Debbie Pedersen's files on the gangbanger. He put them back in the banker's box and walked them over to her desk. While that case was now closed with the death of the only suspect, she might still want to look at it when she got back, although Karb had to wonder if she would come back at all.

Sitting back down at his desk, he looked at the lengthy list of notes he'd want to talk to Capobianco about on her road rage case. He was having trouble concentrating, however, as his thoughts kept returning to the Davies' case. He decided to go for a drive and swing by the scene to get a visual on the house.

The forensics report hadn't come in yet, but Officer Sprehe's report had arrived the day before. Karb had taken it home with him and digested it thoroughly. It confirmed that there might be something there, but nowhere near enough for an arrest.

Crossing the Hawthorne Bridge, he turned on Martin Luther King Boulevard. Going north, he worked his way up to NE Alameda Street. The houses were almost universally large and immaculately landscaped. The Davies' house was a sprawling, stucco house with a two car garage off to the side. It was a corner lot, boundaried by NE Alameda Street and NE Alameda Terrace. There was a low wall along the front with steps leading up from the sidewalk to the front yard and then up to the front door. The landscaping included a combination of new and older, mostly deciduous, trees.

The Davies' house wasn't the largest house in the neighborhood, but it had to be close. Karb estimated it at about four thousand square feet, with the lot being at least a third of an acre. He allowed himself to wonder why any two people would need a house that large.

Karb parked his car just a house away from the Davies' home so as not to attract any attention should Dr. Davies be home. He got out of the car and looked around. There were some landscapers working on a couple of the neighboring homes.

He walked in front of the house directly across the street. It was slightly smaller than the Davies' with more of a classic decor. The garage door was closed, and he walked up the steps toward the front door. He rang the doorbell, but no one answered. The doorbell was one of those newer types with a camera in it. Karb turned around and confirmed that the camera was pointing directly across the street toward the Davies' home.

He made a note to find out who the owners were and request a copy of the doorcam's video. It might not make any difference, but part of being thorough was to obtain any information possible. If Davies did kill his wife, the recording might show some of the interior lights on and that would counter his alibi that he was asleep.

He returned to his car and drove back to the station.

❧

"Bill, I'm glad you're back. The autopsy report just came in."

Karb immediately sat down at his computer and logged in. It only took a few moments to call up the report and he could sense Capobianco watching him. His general procedure was to first do a quick read of the report to get its gist. He would then read it again, taking his time and absorbing more of the details.

"So, we've got some evidence of domestic violence. The bruises on the arm are at least a starting point."

"We all know that simple bruises will never support a finding of DV. There could be any number of reasons why she had those bruises, domestic violence is only one. We'd never be able to prove that Davies even caused them," Capobianco said.

"I know, but we've also got some petechiae clusters around the mouth and nose, as well as around the eyes."

Capobianco again responded, "Yes, but the clusters are small and not solely indicative of any sort of strangulation or suffocation. The broken blood vessels are suggestive at most. Nothing in this report, in and of itself, would support a murder conviction."

"Absolutely," Karb responded, "but it is enough to bring to the captain and start a formal investigation."

Capobianco looked at him and then shrugged. "Okay, let's give it a try. With Meg looking into this, we need to be ready in case something is found by her."

The two detectives got up and walked down the hall to Captain Schnadig's office. Karb waited for Capobianco to knock.

"Come in."

Captain Schnadig was the exact opposite of what some would call a grizzled veteran. He was tall and lean and fastidiously dressed in a three-piece dark suit, with a yellow bowtie and polished black shoes. As they entered, he sat back on his chair with an expectant look on his face.

"Anything new on Debbie?"

"No, sir. We haven't heard anything other than the rumor about the fingerprint."

"It's more than just a rumor. When was the last time you saw her?"

Capobianco responded, "I was with her yesterday. She's being transferred out of the ICU next week. She's still going to be in the hospital a while before she gets transferred to a rehab center. Overall, our friend seems in pretty good spirits, all things considered."

"Capo, she's going to need some counseling to deal with… her injuries. I can't order it at this point," he said, taking a quick look at Karb, "but it would do her good."

"Yes, sir, I'll talk to her. I don't think it will take much encouragement. Debbie is nothing if not practical."

"Good. Now why are you two here?"

Karb spoke up this time, "Captain, as you remember, we were set to see you a couple of weeks ago before the bombing happened with Debbie and Ed Wallace."

The captain nodded his head. "Yes, I remember. What have you got?"

Capobianco then proceeded to summarize what Officer Sprehe had told Karb, noticing the captain's face start getting red when it was explained that the patrolman left the husband alone in the house, other than having an EMT on site, without fully securing the scene.

Karb then spoke up, "Normally, this wouldn't be a priority case given the…errors involved, but then Capo got a call from Meg Nguyen asking about it and whether we were investigating."

The captain sharply banged his hand on his desk. "Goddammit. How the hell did she hear about it?"

He was staring at Capobianco, but she just shrugged her shoulders and held her hands out palms up.

Capobianco spoke up, "Apparently, she got an anonymous phone call suggesting that she check into it. She doesn't know anything more than that, at least as far as we know. She mentioned it on her podcast, however, and we think that we should formally open an investigation…just in case she finds something out there."

"I swear, that woman is going to be the death of me. Alright, let's start looking into this. It is likely that these folks are well-connected, so we don't want to get too far ahead of ourselves. Have you gotten the officer's report or the autopsy results yet?"

Karb handed the captain a copy of the officer's report. "This won't be of much help. The autopsy report at least creates inferences that there were problems between the victim and her husband. There's evidence of DV…"

Capobianco interrupted, "Possible DV."

Karb restarted, "Possible DV and the ME found some burst blood vessels around the mouth, nose, and eyes."

"So, a potential suffocation." The captain stopped and both of the detectives could see him start to put the pieces of the puzzle together. "Wait, she fell down the stairs and *then* was suffocated?"

Karb nodded. "That's the way I'm looking at it, but as Capo will tell you, the evidence isn't as clear as we would like it. The ME's not ready to rule this a homicide yet. The concern is that the petechiae clusters might have been caused by her suffocating from her injuries in falling down the stairs."

"Okay, so what's your next step?"

"Capo located a friend of the vic's, and we're scheduled to meet her tomorrow afternoon. I'd like to meet with the lawyer, Randy Wilkerson, and find out what he can tell me about the vic and the husband."

"Bill, you're not going anywhere near the lawyer. Let's have Capo do that."

"What the hell…why?"

"You and I both know that you don't like lawyers. I know enough about this guy Wilkerson to know that you wouldn't last five minutes before you had your hands around his neck. He'd push every button you have and I'm not ready to have you jeopardize this investigation…or this department."

Karb could feel his face getting flushed. "Captain, I…"

"Bill, this is not up for discussion. You two meet with the vic's friend together. Capo, you'll interview Wilkerson by yourself."

The captain looked at the two detectives.

"Anything else?"

Capobianco and Karb looked at each other and Capobianco shrugged again. She had her hand covering her mouth to hide the smirk. The captain had Karb pegged perfectly, even if he wasn't particularly diplomatic in expressing it.

"Thanks, Cap," Karb said, doing his best to not allow any hint of sarcasm to be part of that comment. The two of them turned and left. Karb walked out the door first and just before she did, Capobianco looked back at the captain. He raised an eyebrow at her and then just nodded his head.

❧

Chapter Fifteen

The house was rundown and in an older neighborhood in Northwest Portland. These were mostly small two-story houses that had been built in the 40's and 50's. This was not the type of neighborhood where there was much pride, if any, in ownership. Lawns were seeded with weeds and often mowed only when the city posted a nuisance notice.

The house that they had identified was missing a couple of shutters and was long overdue to be painted. The picket fence in front had lost all of its color, as well as numerous pickets. There was a faded "Beware of Dog" sign beside the broken gate.

The van was parked just a couple of doors down. Special Agent Michael Merrick waited on the radio. Suddenly it crackled.

"Okay, we've got the back covered. There's one door and no side doors. There's a motorcycle parked in the backyard, but we'll be able to stop anyone who tries to climb on it."

"Good," S.A. Merrick said. "Eby, do you have the south side of the street blocked?"

The response came back immediately. "Affirmative."

"McMahon, do you have the north side blocked?"

"Affirmative."

S.A. Merrick looked at the squad of heavily armed agents in front of him. "Okay, team, it's go time. The thermal imaging indicates that there is only a single person in the house, likely Moody. He is upstairs and in one of the northerly bedrooms. Make sure you knock loudly and identify yourself. I want the neighbors down the street to be able to hear it.

"Be careful, however. We don't know if this guy may have booby-trapped the door. If he doesn't answer, use the flashbangs on all of the windows in the front. If he is going to run, it'll be out the backdoor. Do not, under any circumstances, go inside until I say so. Got it?"

The men and women standing in front of him all nodded.

"Okay, go!"

With that, the agents crossed the street and rushed, in a tight cluster, towards the front of the house. Two agents ran up the stairs. They stood on either side of the front door and one of them banged on it loudly.

"FBI, open up!"

No more than five seconds passed without a response before the agent banged again and yelled, "FBI, open up…now!"

With no response forthcoming, the agent turned to the others in the front yard and gave a hand signal. Those agents immediately threw the flashbang grenades through the front windows on both the first and second floors. The sound of breaking glass was immediately overtaken by the explosions. Even outside of the house, the sound was deafening. The agents were all experienced and had ear protection, quickly averting their eyes from the bright flashes.

Over the radio, S.A. Merrick could hear, "Backdoor! Backdoor!"

The agents in front of the house stayed where they were. In case the thermal imaging had been inaccurate, they wanted to make sure no one was going to try to escape through the front.

Again the radio crackled, and he heard S.A. Kate Eby's voice. "We got him! Repeat, we got him!"

S.A. Merrick let out a deep sigh of relief, not realizing that he had been holding his breath for the last sixty seconds.

Chapter Sixteen

"What did you think?"

Joyce looked at Meg and took a sip of her coffee. She knew that this was just the first episode of their collaboration, so she didn't want to be overly critical. She had known Meg for a long time and while she had a very tough, and even brazen, exterior, she knew Meg could be very fragile. That's the way it often was with people as damaged as Meg.

"Overall, I thought it was good. Your voice was strong. Talking about Debbie Pedersen and the bombing was compelling, but we'll have to see what happens next. The dead socialite doesn't sound like much to me. The co-ed may have some legs, depending on what the autopsy shows and whether any of the rumors of sexual assault at the frat are true.

"These stories, however, just don't seem as compelling as your prior seasons. I loved that second season where you intertwined the stories of the murdered stripper, how her suspected boyfriend was murdered, and then the whole serial killer thing. You had me waiting for each new episode to see what twist would happen next. The unsolved death of the Sorochak guy was puzzling and, I've got to tell you…more than a bit disappointing. Unsolved mysteries won't keep the audience. The next season with the whole Karb story was interesting but not really compelling. Then you had to end it, again, with the unsolved issues involving the death of Sorochak.

"Now, this season, you're setting up three stories and none of them seem particularly…" Joyce looked off in the distance, searching for the right word. Finally, she shrugged her shoulders and merely said, "They're just not sexy. Tragic, yes. Sexy, not really…at least not yet."

Meg was disappointed with Joyce's critique. She understood that she needed this type of independent evaluation if she wanted to improve. Even she recognized that while her show, in the past, had been strong and interesting, it was uneven. That was one of the things that she'd learned in her short time at *20/20*. The stories had to be presented at a relatively steady pace, gradually building to the big reveal that solved the crime and allowed the concept of justice to shine through.

"Yeah, I get it. We could push the car bomb story and I can go more in-depth as to the cop who was killed, as well as Debbie Pedersen. Since the feds are doing the investigation, I don't know that we'll be able to get much inside info from them. I just don't have the contacts there, at least not yet.

"My guess is that they'll identify the bomber fairly quickly. There just aren't a lot of guys out there who know how to build and remotely detonate bombs, especially a fairly sophisticated bomb like was used here. Once they ID the suspect, we can do his background and that might be good. Of course, I don't know how long it's going to take for something to break. I'll knock on some doors to see if Tuna might know of someone with bomb-making expertise."

"Tuna's your contact with the Patriot Boys, right?" Joyce asked.

"Yeah, he's been a pretty good source, and he certainly has his fingers in a lot of different pies around the city. He's never free, though. He always wants information to trade. I'm just not sure I've got anything to trade *with* him at this point."

Joyce took another sip of her coffee. "What about the socialite thing? Should we just let that fade away? I'm not sure there's anything there to grab anyone's attention."

"Joyce, there's something about this case that has my 'spidey-senses' on alert. Part of it is the anonymous call. I also have a feeling about the husband, James Davies. I can't identify it but there's just something about him I don't like. I'm going to do some digging on this. If something turns up, great. Give me a week or so. If it turns cold, we can always drop it."

"Meg, just remember, we have limited resources. Right now, you're our sole investigator and we've already started pushing out product."

"Joyce, I know you didn't want us to start yet but…"

"And if none of these stories pan out," Joyce interrupted harshly, "I will have been right and that won't help either one of us. I know I don't need to remind you that I've pushed all my chips into this hand too, so if this season fails, we both fail. At that point, I'll have to start from scratch with something else. I have no idea what that might be, and I really don't want to think about it."

"Alright, let me do some digging and see what I can find out."

Joyce stood up and drained the last dregs of coffee from her cup. As she walked past Meg, she put her hand on her shoulder and reached down and kissed the top of her head.

"I have faith in you, Meg. You know I do."

"I know," Meg responded, although she wondered how much longer she could rely on that faith lasting.

CHAPTER SEVENTEEN

"How you doing, sunshine? What's shaking?"

Meg stared at the figure in the hospital bed in front of her. Debra Pedersen looked in bad shape. The sheet covering her left leg just dropped to the mattress below the knee. Her head was still wrapped in bandages and her left eye was covered by another. Her hair looked dirty and stringy.

Pedersen struggled to keep her right eye open and focused on Meg. "Not much, what's new with you?" Her voice was slurred and the mere effort to speak caused her to wince in pain.

"Debbie, seriously, how are you doing?"

A tear slowly ran down Pedersen's cheek and she said, very softly, "Distract me! Talk to me about something other than…" she softly waved her right hand across her body, "than this. Lying here forces me to think about…well, to think about things I don't want to think about right now."

Meg sat down next to the hospital bed and softly grasped Pedersen's hand.

"Well, if it helps, I'm trying to figure out whether there's a story about the death of Charlene Price Davies."

Pedersen closed her eye and Meg could tell she was fighting through the fog of the painkillers to place the name.

"The socialite? The doctor's wife who fell down the stairs?"

"Yeah, that's her. Something tells me that there's something there but I'm not sure where to go. Any suggestions?"

Pedersen gave a half-hearted laugh and responded, "I think you're asking the wrong person. I suspect you know as much as I do about that case. Hell, the only thing I was interested in was the chance to talk to Randy Wilkerson."

Meg sat up abruptly but tried not to startle the wounded detective laying on the bed beside her. "Did you learn something about him?"

Meg could tell that Pedersen was starting to fade. "Debbie, what about Wilkerson?"

"Oh, he's apparently a family friend... on both sides. I was going to talk to him but, well I guess Capo is going to have to do it now."

Her voice slowly faded off and Meg tried to revive her. "Debbie? Debbie?"

There was no response other than her soft breathing and the beeping of the heart monitor on the other side of the bed.

Meg stood up and thought to herself that if Wilkerson was somehow involved, this case started having the makings of a sexy story, as Joyce would say. She walked out of the hospital room and sat down in a chair in the hallway.

Taking her phone out, she did a quick internet search and then placed the call.

"Thrower, Kehoe, Wilkerson & Jada, how may I help you?"

Meg quietly said, "May I talk with Mr. Wilkerson's assistant please?'

"Of course, I'll put you through."

Meg only had to wait a couple of seconds before she heard, "Mr. Wilkerson's office, this is LaVonne."

"LaVonne, my name is Jane McKee, I work down at the police station. I understand that Detective Carol Capobianco has an appointment with Mr. Wilkerson, and I need to confirm the date and time."

"Of course, it is this afternoon at 3:00 pm. Will that still work?"

"Gosh, LaVonne, it would really be great if we could push that up an hour. Can you do that for me?"

"Well, let me check. Hmmm, yes, I think we can do that. Should I send a confirming email?"

"No, LaVonne, that won't be necessary. I'll make sure she is there at 2:00 pm on the dot. Thank you so much for your cooperation."

"Of course, and have a good day."

Meg hung up her phone and put it back in her pocket. She looked at her watch and started calculating what to do next.

CHAPTER EIGHTEEN

"So, what do we know about this woman?" Karb asked. "Her name is Michelle Polidori, in her late forties, divorced twice, current husband is a much older property developer, mid-seventies. She seems to be a local celebrity wannabe. She shows up regularly on the social pages. Most importantly for us is that she was apparently Charlene Davies' best friend and they have been close since high school."

The elevator door opened and Karb motioned for Capobianco to enter first. She pushed the button for the garage.

"She should be able to give us some background on both Charlene and Dr. Davies. If there's any dirt there, she should know about it. We just have to make sure that she'll tell us about it. I've printed out some fluff pieces from the Oregonian for you, as well as a couple of pages from her Facebook page. That should give you a feel for her."

Capobianco handed him a thin manila folder and led him to her car. They both got in and she started driving up the ramp leading to S.W. 2nd Avenue. Karb concentrated on reading the printouts and it was only a ten-minute drive before they pulled into the parking garage for the Multnomah Athletic Club.

They took the stairs down to the main level, crossed S.W. Salmon Street and moved toward the double glass doors that were the entrance into the eight-story behemoth. The Multnomah Athletic Club was the city's premier health and social club. With four different restaurants, multiple ballrooms, a swimming pool, tennis, basketball, squash, and other courts, all spread out over six hundred thousand square feet, the MAC Club was dripping with both money and prestige. The initiation fee, not to mention the monthly dues, was far beyond the budget of most Portlanders.

If you were amongst Portland's upper class or if you had any political aspirations, a membership at the MAC was almost a prerequisite, perhaps not as much as thirty years previously, but it was still a place for Portland's movers and shakers to see and be seen.

As they approached the glass doors, a young man in khakis and a button-down light blue shirt opened the door for them and wished them a good afternoon. Heading toward the front desk, both detectives took note of the large lobby. It was a three-story atrium with leather couches and walnut woodwork. The sun shining through the clear roof gave it an appearance of an upscale office building more than just a health club.

Walking up to the front desk, Capobianco put her hand on the well-polished desk and addressed the young woman standing there. She was also wearing a pair of khaki pants and blue button-down shirt, albeit unlike the boy at the door, she had a thin gold necklace on and a tennis bracelet. The diamonds on the bracelet sparkled in the sunshine.

Looking down at her name tag, Capobianco started, "Ashley, I'm Detective Carol Capobianco, and this is my partner, Detective Bill Karb. We are with the Portland Police Department and have an appointment with one of your members…Michelle Polidori."

"Of course, Ma'am. Let me just check our schedule."

Ashley started typing on the keyboard in front of her.

"Oh, here we go. Mrs. Polidori is up on the Sunset Bistro." Looking over Karb's shoulder, she called out to another young man wearing the same MAC uniform. "Calvin, can you escort these detectives up to the sun deck? They have a meeting with Mrs. Polidori."

"Of course, Ashley." Looking at the detectives, he said, "Good afternoon, if you'll follow me, I'll take you up to the Bistro."

Capobianco and Karb looked at each other and both of them started shaking their head in wonder at all of the pomp and formality for what was, at its heart, a gym.

The ride to the eighth floor was quick and when the door opened, Calvin led them around the corner and out onto a sun-drenched patio with no more than fifteen tables. Just past the tables was a railing and, just beyond that, Karb could see the pitch used by the Portland Timbers and Thorns professional soccer teams. The pitch was surround by stadium seating on three sides, with the fourth side being the MAC building.

This was a classic early spring day with the trees in the distance and throughout the West Hills starting to turn a bright green. They continued to follow the staffer as he led them to a table where a single, middle-aged woman was frantically typing on her iPhone.

"Mrs. Polidori?" the staffer asked.

Before they could introduce themselves, the woman stood up from the table and in a voice louder than was necessary exclaimed, "You must be Detective Bill Karb. Oh, Detective, I am so pleased to meet you."

She reached out her hand to Karb and he shook it without a word. The two detectives sat down across from her. Michelle Polidori appeared to be a little older than her biography suggested. She was slender, almost gaunt, and her makeup and hair looked as if they had been professionally done just for this meeting.

Polidori looked at Capobianco and said, in a much lower voice, "And who might you be?"

Capobianco took a breath and extended her hand. "I'm Detective Carol Capobianco. It's nice to meet you."

Polidori listlessly shook the offered hand and faced Karb. In a voice, again slightly louder than necessary, she said, "Detective Karb, I am probably your biggest fan. Oh, I should ask, am I being investigated for something?"

Karb took a quick look around; it was clear that this woman wanted to make sure that they were seen. For her, she obviously wanted to be seen with him. Her fawning over him made him uncomfortable.

"No, you're not. Mrs. Polidori, we have just…"

Reaching over to put her hand on top of his, she interrupted, "Please, call me Michelle. I'm not a particularly formal person."

Karb sensed that this was a lie and all part of the act she was putting on for everyone watching. People were still talking, but doing so quietly enough so they could still eavesdrop.

Capobianco started, "Mrs. Polidori, we understand you were friends with Charlene Davies."

Polidori briefly turned her head toward Capobianco but then looked back at Karb. She reached into her purse and pulled out a handkerchief. Dabbing her eyes, she responded to Karb, "Oh yes, poor Char. This is just so, so sad."

She continued to wipe her eyes with the handkerchief for all to see.

"How long had you known her?" Capobianco made another attempt to steer the questioning, even though she was apparently invisible to this woman.

"Oh, Char and I go back to high school at Catlin Gable. Bill… may I call you Bill?"

Karb nodded his head yes.

"Char was always the prettiest and sweetest girl. I just can't believe she's gone."

"What year did the two of you graduate?" Karb asked this, realizing that he was going to have to take over the questioning. Out of the corner of his eye, he saw Capobianco break out a smile and shake her head.

Polidori's cheeks flushed at the question, and she leaned in and practically whispered, "1983."

Trying to hide his smirk, Karb continued, "And, you remained friends since then?"

"Bill," Polidori replied, "Char and I have been best friends forever. I was even the maid of honor in her first marriage. Oh, that poor woman went through so much."

"What can you tell me about her first marriage…it was to Ken Price, wasn't it?"

"Oh, Ken was such a fabulous man. You know, don't you, that he was one of the early executives at Nike." This was a rhetorical question, so Karb just nodded his head. "He was funny and so, *so* handsome. They made such a wonderful couple and a beautiful family. I'm godmother to their daughter, you know."

Again, Karb nodded his head and jotted down a note on his pad.

"It was so sad when he died."

"How did he pass?" The detectives already knew the answers to most of these questions. Nonetheless, they found it helpful to ask these types of questions in order to be able to gauge the truthfulness of a witness for purposes of other, more important, questions.

"Oh, he went in for what was to be a simple bypass operation on his heart. You would have thought that someone at Nike would exercise regularly, but the only exercising Ken ever did was climbing in and out of his golf cart. Shame on me, that was mean! I should know better than to speak ill of the dead. Please excuse me. He was such a lovely man, and he died far too young."

"So, what happened?"

"Well, Char told me that they were unable to get his heart restarted. It was apparently far more diseased than the cardiologist expected. She was told that it was unusual but not unheard of."

"When did this happen?"

"It was six years ago. Little Kelly was only twelve and she was devastated. She was such a daddy's girl. I spent so much time at their house, just trying to console and support the both of them."

"Would you say they had a good marriage?"

"Oh, they were the best couple ever. They were wonderful together. Thank goodness Ken took care of her financially. I don't know the exact amount, but between the life insurance and his stock options, Char was able to maintain a proper lifestyle. I mean she had a little money of her own, but Portland can be so expensive these days. Her daughter even attended Catlin Gable, just like we did."

"Michelle, that is truly unfortunate about Mr. Price. Can you tell us how is it that Charlene came to meet and marry Dr. Davies? Were they friends?"

"Oh, heavens no. They had a mutual friend in Randy Wilkerson. Do you know Randy?"

Capobianco raised an eyebrow at the mention of the lawyer.

"I've heard of him."

"Oh, my, isn't he amazing?" Lowering her head and finally taking notice of Capobianco, she quietly said, "If we weren't friends…well, let's just say Randy and I would know each other much better." She let out a short laugh that was almost the type you would expect from a young schoolgirl.

Sitting up and taking a sip of her iced tea, she composed herself and continued, "Randy was great to her. He's managed her trust since Ken died."

"What trust is that?"

"Ken set up a trust for Char and Kelly before he died. Char is…I mean *was* a wonderful woman, but she just wasn't very good with finances. Ken figured that Randy would be the one to make sure that Char and Kelly were taken care of.

"Char thought the world of Randy. I always thought those two would get together but, instead, it was her and Jim." She practically spit out Davies' name.

"Michelle, do I detect that you're not the biggest fan of Dr. Davies?"

Karb could see Polidori stop and think about how to respond.

"Jim is alright, but he really isn't…well, he just isn't one of us. Sure, he's a doctor but he never seemed to have much money and always had Char pay for things. Also, he could be a bit crass and seemed to hate socializing. Even worse, he just wasn't affectionate to Char like Ken had been. Char wouldn't admit it, but I think she knew she might have made a mistake. Jim was pretty charming at first but once they got married, he just started acting strange. He didn't want to take her to parties or even out to dinner. She often went to functions alone and would tell people that Jim wasn't feeling well. Everybody knew though. Sometimes she would convince Randy to escort her to dinner parties and other formal functions. You know, they made a gorgeous couple, Randy and Char."

"Might there have been anything more between Charlene and Mr. Wilkerson?"

Again, Polidori blushed and took a long sip of her iced tea. She looked around and then softly replied, "Bill, is it important? I don't like to be the one to spread gossip, even if I think it's true. Wait," she said, her voice getting slightly louder, "do you think Jim might have killed her?"

Karb responded immediately in his own soft voice. "Michelle, all we're trying to do is confirm that Char's death was just an accident. This is all standard background."

She stared at Karb and even took a quick glance at Capobianco to figure out what, and how much, to say.

"So might there have been a romantic relationship between Charlene and Wilkerson?"

"Is this confidential? I don't want anyone to know that I might have told you anything."

Karb thought this was a bit disingenuous, given how she had orchestrated this whole public appearance, but nodded. "We can make this off the record." In the world of criminal investigations, there was no such thing, but Karb knew that Polidori either wouldn't know that or wouldn't really care.

Still leaning slightly over the table, Michelle started, "Char confided in me that she and Jim had problems…in the bedroom, if you know what I mean."

Karb nodded his head.

"They were even sleeping in separate bedrooms for the last couple of years. I know she also didn't like the way that he disciplined Kelly. It wasn't just in comparison to Ken that Jim failed as a stepfather. He was just mean to Kelly. He was very conservative and didn't approve of her behavior. It was almost like he was trying to drive a wedge between Char and Kelly.

"Understand, she wasn't a wild kid, but her dad had died, and she had a lot of friends. Char even told me that she thought Kelly might be experimenting with drugs. I know all kids experiment, but Jim was absolutely opposed to drugs of any kind. Kind of ironic, isn't it, given that he's an anesthesiologist? Anyway, I'm sure that is why Kelly insisted on going to school up at Washington and so rarely comes home. She just doesn't want to be around him."

Polidori stopped as a waiter came by and refilled her iced tea. When he walked away, she continued, "Oh, I'm sorry, I went off on a bit of a tangent. About a year or so ago, I noticed Char was starting to act strangely. She was happier than I had seen her in a long time. I finally confronted her and asked if she was having an affair. She tried to deny it, but she eventually broke and admitted it. She wouldn't tell me who, but you could tell that she was starved for love and this man, whoever he was, filled that need. This wasn't one of those sordid little trysts, she was madly in love."

"With whom?"

"She wouldn't tell me. Trust me, I tried. Char could be very discreet when she wanted to and apparently, she really wanted to be. She would tell Jim that she was involved in various non-profits and had to attend board meetings and even retreats to explain her being gone and meeting up with the mystery man. The schmuck never had a clue."

"Was this still going on when she died?"

"No, about two weeks before she passed, Char told me that she was going to break it off with the mystery man and try to work on her marriage. She wouldn't tell me why or whether something had happened with her paramour, but she seemed sincere in trying to work things out with Jim. They even went to marriage counseling."

"Did that seem to help?"

"Char wouldn't say but she didn't have the same spark she used to have when she was married to Ken or involved with her paramour. Jim is just such an odd and unlikeable man."

"Is it possible that he knew about her affair?"

"I don't think so. As I said, Char was very discreet but, I don't know, I guess he might have figured it out."

"So do you think she might have been having the affair with Wilkerson?"

Polidori sat back and seemed to really think about it. "I wondered the same thing for a long time, but I really don't think so. They were very good friends, but it almost seemed more of a brother-sister relationship than anything else."

Capobianco then asked, "Did you ever see Dr. Davies get violent with Char?"

"Absolutely not. Char wouldn't have put up with that. He could be verbally and emotionally abusive when he got angry, but I've never known him to be physical. Char was always very vain about her looks, but then again, who isn't? He would tell her that she was getting fat or point out some wrinkles. He could just be so damn mean."

"Michelle, I'm going to ask you a very delicate question."

Polidori nodded her head. "Okay."

"Do you think it's possible that Dr. Davies might have pushed Char down the stairs?"

This time Polidori looked over the railing at the playing field of Providence Park. The Portland Timbers were holding a practice and she just watched for a minute or so. Turning back to him, she took another sip of her iced tea and said, "Maybe."

Chapter Nineteen

The receptionist looked at her watch and then across at the woman fidgeting on the leather chair in the law firm's lobby.

"Detective Capobianco, I'm sure Mr. Wilkerson will be ready to meet with you at any moment. I know he's been very busy lately."

"That's fine, I'll give him another five minutes and then we can arrange to meet down at the police station."

Just then, a middle-aged Black woman came out. "Detective Capobianco?" The woman stopped for a moment and then continued, "I'm LaVonne Floyd, Mr. Wilkerson's legal assistant. Would you like to come with me?"

"Yes, thank you." There was more than a hint of annoyance in her voice. She followed Mrs. Floyd down the hall and into a very large, very plush office. She looked around and noted the remarkable view from the twentieth floor overlooking the Willamette River. The top of Mt. Hood stood out above some low hanging clouds. Despite her continued annoyance at being kept waiting, she had to admit to being impressed.

"Mr. Wilkerson should be with you momentarily, Detective."

She barely had time to get comfortable in one of the soft leather chairs directly in front of Wilkerson's sleek glass desk when she heard the faint sound of a toilet flush and a door she hadn't realized was even there opened. Wilkerson was still drying his hands as he strode across the room to her.

"Excuse me for the delay, as well as my damp hands. Detective Capobianco, I assume?"

"Please, just call me Carol." Up close, she could truly appreciate what an amazingly handsome man he was. The photographs in the newspapers didn't do him justice. He approached her with a grace that suggested he was either an athlete or a dancer…or both. Rather than walk behind his desk, he pulled out the other leather chair next to hers and held out his hand.

She took his hand and marveled at how soft his skin was. Clearly, he had never done a moment of manual labor in his life.

"Detective Capobianco, I'm so sorry…Carol, again I'm sorry for keeping you waiting. Has my assistant offered you something to drink?" She could feel his eyes aggressively examining every square inch of her body. A slight blush came to her cheeks.

She looked over his shoulder and could see Mrs. Floyd back at her desk. She wasn't sure if she felt comfort or disappointment in knowing they wouldn't be alone.

"No, but that's fine. I just want to ask you a few questions about Charlene Davies."

Wilkerson looked down and shook his head.

"Such a tragedy. We had been friends for a long time. In fact, I've been a longtime friend with her entire family."

"Yes, I've heard that. I just want to ask a few questions about her."

"Please understand, Carol, Char was both a client and a friend. I'm more than willing to talk about what she may have told me as a friend, but I'm barred from disclosing any information she may have provided to me as her attorney."

She stared at him for a moment and tried to read what was going on behind the gorgeous eyes.

"Of course, Mr. Wilkerson, I'm not seeking any privileged information, just some basic background."

"Now it's my turn, please just call me Randy."

He had a disarming smile that she knew must be effective on just about everyone he met. She'd have to be very careful not to fall for it.

"Randy, I understand that in addition to friendship with Mrs. Davies, you've known Dr. Davies a long time, even before he married Charlene."

She watched as he stiffened slightly and only momentarily.

"I am, I've known Jim since college. I feel so sorry for him, losing the love of your life like that. Are you married Carol?"

She chuckled slightly and shook her head from side to side.

"So, I understand that you set up a trust for Mrs. Davies and her first husband. Is that correct?"

"Carol, you're getting into areas..."

She cut him off. "Randy, I'm not asking for specifics about the trust. Whether you set up a trust or not does not involve the attorney-client privilege."

Wilkerson sat back, slowly raised his right hand, and examined his recently manicured fingernails. Gradually he lowered his hands and returned his gaze to the woman in front of him.

"Yes, I did, as a matter of fact. Actually, I had a former associate of mine prepare it."

"Former?"

"Yes, the young man wasn't very thorough. He made some mistakes with the trust that we didn't catch. I guess we assumed that he was more qualified than he turned out to be."

"What kind of mistakes?"

"I'm sorry, Carol, but I don't feel comfortable disclosing that information without my client's consent."

"And who would your client be at this point?"

Wilkerson again fidgeted slightly, almost imperceptibly, in his chair before responding, "The trustee of the trust." He wasn't used to being interrogated and this Detective Capobianco was very skilled at it.

"And who would that be?"

Wilkerson was starting to get agitated. "I'm sorry, Detective, but I don't think I can share that information with you."

Leaning in slightly, she said, "Randy, I'm not a lawyer but I have it on pretty good authority that this was likely a revocable trust that became irrevocable on the death of Ken Price and/or Charlene Davies."

She stopped and looked at him for a moment and then continued, "If it did convert to an irrevocable trust, you'll be filing tax returns. In those returns, you'll have to disclose the name of the current trustee. Would you agree that by filing a return with the IRS and the State, any attorney-client privilege as to the identity of the trustee is waived?"

Wilkerson took a breath. "Of course, Carol. I'm impressed, you've done your homework. The fact of the matter is that I am the trustee and have been since Ken's death."

Any feelings of awe or intimidation she might have experienced when she first shook hands with Wilkerson were now gone. She realized that he was just a lawyer—a gorgeous lawyer, but just a lawyer nonetheless, and not one above playing games.

"So, with that, you are effectively wearing two hats—one as the lawyer for the trust and the other being the trustee."

Wilkerson nodded but did not respond.

"The attorney-client privilege applies to any communications you have with your clients as to establishing the trust but while you are serving as a trustee, there is no privilege between any communications you may have, as the trustee, with Dr. Davies and/or Mrs. Davies. Do I have that correct?"

"Carol, it is a very gray area and if you are going to ask for specific communications with either Jim or Char, I think I should consult with *my* attorney before answering. Do you understand?"

"Oh, certainly, Randy, I get that. So, as the trustee and not as a lawyer, tell me what mistakes your former associate made on this trust."

Wilkerson realized that he was being outmaneuvered, something that only happened rarely, and never by a policewoman. He gave his most charming smile and said, "Carol, how about if we talk in generalities, rather than about this particular trust? That way I can answer some of your questions without having to get my attorney involved."

Waiting for the woman to confirm her consent, he watched as she nodded and then continued, "Generally, when I set up a trust for a married couple, I set it up so that when the first person dies, the trust estate is split into two separate trusts. I won't bore you with the tax ramifications but let's just say that I usually refer to them as a decedent's trust and a survivor's trust.

"The decedent's trust becomes irrevocable, and the beneficiaries can't make any material changes to that trust. The other trust, the survivor's trust, remains revocable and the survivor can do with it what he or she wants. The surviving beneficiary can even dissolve the trust and give it all to a charity or put it all on black at the roulette tables in Vegas if that is what the survivor desires to do."

She could sense that he was trying to both impress and charm her. He wasn't being successful with either, so she just nodded.

"If a now-former associate erred by failing to draft a trust to allow for the decedent's trust to become irrevocable upon the death of the first spouse, the surviving beneficiary would then be able to change the names of the secondary beneficiaries."

Speaking up quickly, she said, "So the decedent's trust remained revocable, and Char changed the secondary beneficiary from who to who? Did she remove her daughter as a beneficiary and name Dr. Davies?"

"Detective, as I told you, I'm only willing to talk in generalities until I'm able to consult with my attorney."

He had a smirk on his face that she found very unattractive.

She responded, "So, if in this hypothetical case, a child was cut out of the trust, she might be very upset about that former associate's mistake."

Wilkerson didn't like this statement and chose not to respond.

"By the way, have you spoken with Kelly Price?"

"As a matter of fact, Detective, I met with her just a couple of days ago."

"And did you explain to her the mistake that your former associate made in the drafting of the trust agreement?"

Wilkerson leaned forward. "Detective, you are starting to wear on my patience. What I do and do not disclose to a client or other interested party is between me and that person. I can assure you that we here at the firm understand all of our ethical obligations and fully and completely comply with them."

He looked down and smoothed out the wrinkles on the thighs of his slacks.

"I'm sorry, Detective, but I think we're done talking about this. I've got a meeting coming up in a few minutes."

Wilkerson stood up and casually stretched out his legs and again smoothed out the wrinkles with his hands.

"LaVonne," he called through the door. His assistant appeared immediately. "Please show Detective Capobianco out."

"Randy, it was nice to meet you. If I have further questions, may I call you?"

"Detective, I have to say that your questions started to border on being insulting. Let's just say that I won't be available until you hand me a subpoena. Fair enough?"

She smiled, "Fair enough," then turned and followed the assistant out the door.

Once they were down the hall and out of earshot of Wilkerson's office, the assistant stopped and reached for her hand. "It was a pleasure to meet you Ms. Nguyen. I'm a big fan."

Meg felt something solid being passed to her.

"Thank you, LaVonne."

"You're welcome and if I can be of any assistance in the future, please let me know." She then reached into a pocket and retrieved a business card. "My cell phone number is on the back."

Meg looked at the woman in front of her and smiled.

"I'll do that. I will certainly do that."

Meg then nodded her head and walked out the door. She stopped and turned back to the assistant. "LaVonne, do you know the approximate value of the Price trust?"

LaVonne looked around to make sure no one could hear. "According to the last annual accounting, it was slightly under forty million dollars."

Meg's head involuntarily twisted to the side. "Really?"

LaVonne nodded her head.

"Well, this case just gets more and more interesting." Meg then turned and just as she reached the elevator, the door opened, and she stepped in. She tried to remember every detail of her meeting with Wilkerson and, perhaps more importantly, Mrs. LaVonne Floyd. She mindlessly tossed the memory stick between her hands and wondered what she might find on it.

The elevator came to a smooth stop at the lobby level and the doors opened.

"Meg? Meg! What are you doing here?"

Meg gave Carol Capobianco a hug and responded, "Oh, I'm just doing some research."

Capobianco leaned in close and whispered into Meg's ear, "I've got a meeting with the Silver Fox. Give me a call later and I'll fill you in."

Meg gave her a warm smile and said, "Good luck, Capo. I look forward to hearing all about it."

Meg was looking forward to their conversation. Capobianco would be pissed and accuse her of impersonating a police officer, but Meg never crossed the line. She may have told Wilkerson to call her "Carol" but never claimed to be a police officer or identified herself as a detective. She may have led them all, from the receptionist to Wilkerson, to assume that was who she was but had been very careful not to cross that line.

Capobianco would forgive her once she was given a copy of whatever was on the memory stick, although that was going to involve some give-and-take.

The first step would be to examine the documents on the memory stick and then discuss strategy with Joyce.

☙

CHAPTER TWENTY

"Mike, when they come in, I strongly recommend that you say nothing. Let me do the talking. If they make an offer, you and I can discuss it later. They'll try and press you to make a decision right away but don't. They'll only make an offer if they think you have something that they want. Whatever that is, they'll still want it tomorrow so don't let them…"

There was a loud knock on the door, and it immediately opened. The first person through the door was a tall, middle-aged woman. She had brown hair with just a few streaks of gray and was wearing a dark pantsuit. Following her was an older man in a rumpled suit.

The woman spoke first. "Counselor, Mr. Moody, my name is Leslie Westfall, I'm the Deputy US Attorney for Oregon. This is my colleague Harald Kohl."

She sat down directly across from Moody and Kohl settled in beside her. Westfall placed a file on the table in front of her and opened it. She studied it for a moment before looking up at Moody.

"Mike, here's the deal. You're being charged with two counts of first-degree murder, one count of attempted murder, terrorism, and various other federal crimes. I have no doubt that we'll seek the death penalty. Even if we can't get that, you'll spend the rest of your life in a maximum-security prison. This isn't even a close case. We found a palm print of yours on the bomb casing and we know of your history as a munition's specialist in the Marines. We also know your criminal record since you were discharged."

"Leslie…" Moody's public defender began to speak.

"Don't," Westfall said forcefully. "Don't talk, counsel. I'm telling your client what is going to happen to him. You can counsel him as much as you want when I'm done, but I won't have you interrupt me and waste my time."

Deputy US Attorney Westfall then turned back to Moody. "Mike, I know you spent some time in state prison, but if you don't already know this, there is a big difference between state and federal penitentiaries. You are going to do hard time for the next thirty years or however long you last in there.

"These prisons are full of the worst of the worst, all of whom are just looking for a distraction from the monotony of prison life. At best, you'll become somebody's fuck buddy and only loaned out on special occasions. At worst, you'll be beaten and raped more times than you can possibly count.

"You'll likely be shipped far enough away that you'll rarely, if ever, see your wife and children again, other than an occasional photo.

"This isn't a threat. This is just the reality of your situation. I have a proposal for you, however. I suspect that you were hired by the Hoover Street gang to kill Arriaza and maybe even Ed Wallace, Portland's gang enforcement captain. You'll tell me everything I want to know about the Hoover Street Gang.

"I also know you work with the Patriot Boys. You're going to tell me everything you know about them, as well. You'll also testify against any of them we choose to prosecute in the future. Assuming you cooperate, we'll provide you with some additional protection in prison and, after ten years and assuming you behave yourself in there, we'll get you transferred to a medium security prison.

"I'll tell you, it's not much better but you'll be able to have some semblance of a life. In Max, you'll spend a minimum of twenty hours a day in your solitary cell. You'll be safe there during those twenty hours, but those other four hours will be hell. In medium-security, you'll get time in the yard where you can at least get some sunshine and do whatever the fuck type of exercise you want. We'll also transfer you to Sheridan so your wife and kids can visit you.

"That's the deal. You talk and you can have at least some sort of life. You turn it down and you're fucked."

Westfall closed the file in front of her and stared at the criminal in front of her.

"What's it going to be, Mike?"

The legal defender spoke up, "Ms. Westfall, thanks for the offer. We'll think about it."

Westfall slammed her hand on the table. "No! This deal is for now. Either accept it immediately or I'm done, and we'll see you crushed by life in a max prison. This is a one-time offer. As soon as I walk out that door, the offer is gone. What is it going to be?"

Just then there was a knock on the door, and everyone looked up. The door slowly opened, and a guard ushered a stylish young woman into the room. Looking only at Westfall, she said, "Counsel, I'm Annie Hegedus. I'm Mr. Moody's new attorney."

She then looked at the public defender and said, "You're excused. Thanks for whatever you've done. I'll take it from here."

Hegedus then stared at the public defender as he gathered his file, placed it in his briefcase, and stood up. Looking at his now-former client, he asked, "Mike, are you sure about this?"

Hegedus, not waiting for Moody to respond, simply replied, "He's sure."

She continued to stare at the public defender until he left, and the guard closed the door. Hegedus then handed her card to Leslie Westfall and said, "I'm going to talk to my client and then I'll call you tomorrow."

"Counsel, no, that's not the way it works. I've made your client a one-time offer that expires when I walk out of this room."

"Okay," Hegedus responded.'

"Okay what?"

"Okay, the offer expires. Now, may I talk with my client in private?"

"You don't want to even hear the specifics of the offer?" Westfall asked.

"No."

The two women stared at one another. There is a natural antipathy between prosecutors and defense attorneys but what both attorneys were feeling at that point was much more than that. They both recognized that each of them had a dominant personality and neither liked the other.

Westfall stood up, followed by her assistant Kohl. "Fair enough, counsel, see you in Court."

"I'm sure you will," Hegedus responded and then sat down in the chair previously taken by the public defender. She didn't bother to look up as Westfall left the room. Once the door latched, she pulled a small black device from her briefcase.

"Who are you?" Moody inquired.

Rather than verbally responding, Hegedus put a single finger to her lips to signify that he should be quiet. She then stood up and, holding the device in front of her, walked around the room and then waved it across the table.

"Good, there are no listening devices," she said.

"Listening devices? I thought conversations with an attorney were confidential."

"Mike, listen, I don't trust anybody or anything. Not all law enforcement can be trusted to play by the rules. I'm going to make this as quick as possible. I've got other clients I need to meet with. I've been asked by Tuna to represent you."

"Why would Tuna get me an attorney? This job didn't involve him."

"No shit it didn't involve him. You should've known better than to take on a job off the books and not clear it with him first. You're lucky that the Feds got to you before he did."

"Why's Tuna pissed at me?"

"Shut up, Mike. He's pissed because of what the prosecutor just offered you. Let me guess, she wants you to testify against Tuna and the Patriot Boys, as well as those shitheads who hired you for that hit."

Moody looked at her, then lowered his head due to the intensity of her gaze.

"Yeah," was all he could get out.

"And she told you that if you don't, she was going to seek the death penalty, which is bullshit, but that you'll likely spend the rest of your life in max prison as someone's cell block bitch. Is that pretty much what she said?"

Moody was still looking at his shoes and gave a quiet "yes" in response.

"Well, Mike, this is your lucky day. I'm going to tell you the truth about what is going to happen. You are at a fork in the road. One path involves cooperating with the Feds and telling them everything you know about the Patriot Boys and whatever shitheel gang hired you. That is certainly one choice you have.

"You should know, however, that if that is your choice, Tuna is going to be very unhappy. I don't know what he might do but am fairly certain that you wouldn't last a month in prison. More importantly, your two kids, your mom, and even your little brother may very well end up missing. Mike, look at me."

She waited for him to slowly raise his head.

"I'm telling you this, not as any sort of threat, but as your attorney. It is important for me to counsel you on the consequences of your decisions. Your short life in prison will involve repeated and very violent rapes. You can't imagine what that will be like. Do you understand what I just explained to you?"

She could barely hear his affirmative response.

"Good, now I mentioned that this is like a fork in the road, and you have another path you can take. The second road involves you refusing to talk about Tuna and the Patriot Boys at all. He doesn't care what you tell them about the Hoover Street assholes, but Tuna *does* care about what you might say about him and your old friends.

"If you protect them, he'll make sure you are taken care of in prison. You won't be anyone's bitch…unless you want to be. Tuna tells me that he's got connections with various Aryan groups in every max prison across the country and can pull in some favors. Even better, he'll make sure that your boys can go to college if they want to.

"I don't know about you but that sounds like a pretty good deal to me. What do you think, Mike?"

Moody placed his elbows on the table in front of him and buried his head in his hands. He had to stifle the tears.

"Look, you fucked up big time and now you're going to have to pay the price. The only question for you is how much of a price you and your loved ones are ready to pay. I'm going now, but I'll be back to talk to you in a couple of days. I strongly recommend that you not talk to anyone while you're here. Your cellies will sell you out in a heartbeat if they can, so keep your mouth shut. If I find out that you've talked to anyone, including a fed, I'll assume you've made the wrong choice. At that point, I'll resign as your attorney, and I'll wish you luck because you're going to need it.

"Otherwise, when we next meet, you'll tell me that you've agreed to Tuna's offer, and I'll then start negotiating with the Feds. Got it?"

"Yeah, I got it. There's no way to negotiate a lighter sentence?

"Are you fucking nuts? You killed a cop and almost killed another. There is nothing but life inside for you. The only questions will be how long and difficult that life will be. Jesus, how the hell did you not consider this possibility when you agreed to this hit?"

Annie Hegedus didn't wait for a response but, rather, stood up and grabbed her briefcase. She knocked on the door and when it opened, she walked out. She didn't bother acknowledging the sobs emanating from her client.

Moody sat there experiencing that odd sensation that some people feel when there are no positive options. No matter what decision he made, his life, as he knew it, was effectively over. He'd spent time in prison before but always for definite terms and always in a state penitentiary. Now he had no hope for release. He understood the options and realized that there really was only one. At the very least, he owed it to his wife and kids to take care of them.

Standing up, he walked over to the closest wall. It was hardened cinderblock and Moody started banging his head against it as hard as he could. He only stopped when the guards came in and forcibly restrained him.

CHAPTER TWENTY-ONE

Karb looked at his watch. It wasn't like Capobianco to be late, and he wondered if she might have swung by the rehab center to check on Pedersen. He reminded himself that he needed to do that too. Dr. Malone would want him to, and he'd like to visit his friend without being told that he should.

While lost in his thoughts, he didn't notice Capobianco stomping into the office, so he was startled when she threw her purse on her desk and exclaimed, "God damn her!"

He wasn't used to seeing her this angry. He'd seen her frustrated before, as well as being upset and occasionally emotional but never completely pissed off like this. It was usually he who was angry, so he found this change in dynamics somewhat amusing. Doing his best to keep the smirk off his face, he asked with feigned sweetness, "Good morning, Capo, what's shaking?"

Detective Capobianco gave him a stare that suggested he was lucky she did not have a knife in her hand. Now a sly smirk was starting to appear.

"That fucking bitch! I can't believe she did that to me."

Karb rarely called her 'Carol', generally preferring to just call her Capo. In this moment, however, he realized that using her first name would drive her crazy. It was not his nature to tease people, but he was beginning to understand why some people enjoyed it.

"*Carol,* is it safe to assume you're not talking about Debbie?"

"Fuck you, Bill, and wipe that fucking grin off your face!"

She sat down and repeatedly squeezed and loosened her fists, while slowing her breath.

"I almost called you yesterday afternoon but, well, I just really didn't want to talk to you."

"Well, that's sounds fair enough. So, what's got you all riled up this lovely morning?"

"That fucking Meg. She screwed us over."

Karb sat up straight. He knew that Meg and Capo were friends, so Meg must have done something big to get Capo this upset.

"You know how I was supposed to talk to Wilkerson yesterday afternoon?"

"Yeah, what happened?"

"Well, I got there, and his assistant said that he had already met with Detective Carol Capobianco and that Wilkerson was now out at a client meeting. I showed her my badge and I finally figured out that Meg had pretended to be me and questioned Wilkerson. The assistant said that she had pissed him off and that it was unlikely that he'd voluntarily speak with me."

Karb nodded and said, "Interesting, impersonating a police officer is a felony. Maybe it's time we clipped her wings a bit. What do you think?"

Capobianco loved the idea, other than the fact that it would make her and the whole department look like fools. It wouldn't take much to push the captain over the edge when it came to Meg, and she wasn't sure if she was ready to do that…yet.

There was a knock on the wall just behind Capobianco's desk. "I've got a peace offering."

Standing there was Meg with three cups of coffee from Starbucks. Capobianco stood up, looking as if she was ready to punch her.

"Calm down, Capo. I know I kind of screwed you over, but you'll be glad when I tell you what I've got for you."

"Screwed me over? Goddammit Meg, you impersonated a police officer. I'm just trying to decide when to arrest you."

"Capo, I did not technically impersonate you. I never identified myself as you or any other police officer. Wilkerson and his assistant made certain assumptions when I announced that I was there to meet with Wilkerson. When he addressed me, I specifically told him to call me Carol. I never held myself out as you. At worst, I merely implied I was you and allowed them to draw an incorrect inference."

Capobianco was still standing there, her face completely flushed.

"Meg," Bill interjected, trying to ease Capobianco's anger, "you said you have something for us. I assume that *something* isn't just the overpriced coffee you're holding."

Meg maneuvered around Capobianco and sat down in a chair that Karb had pulled out. She placed the coffee on his desk and then reached into her pocket and pulled out a memory stick.

"This, my friends, is the Price Family Revocable Trust Agreement, with all addenda. Do you want to know what it says?"

Karb nodded, while Capobianco sat down and glared at her.

"Well, Charlene Davies' first husband set up a very large trust for her and their daughter. Wilkerson screwed up in drafting the trust agreement, which allowed Charlene to amend the trust shortly before she died. As a result of this amendment, her new husband, Dr. James Davies, became the principal beneficiary should she die. I can't imagine how he convinced her to screw over her own daughter, but it looks like he did. This," she said, waving the memory stick in the air, "gives you motive. You now have motive, means, and opportunity.

"Capo, I know you're angry, but you would never have gotten this from Wilkerson."

"And how did you get it?" Karb asked.

"Bill, I'd love to share that information with you, but I've got to protect my sources."

She looked at Capobianco with a pleased smile on her face, but noted that while she was no longer flushed, she was still pissed off.

"Capo, I've got some more work to do but I hope you can review this gift and, with a little reflection, forgive me. I'm not proud of what I did but this was an opportunity I couldn't pass up."

"How did you even know I was scheduled to meet with Wilkerson?"

"Sorry, Capo. I've got to protect *all* of my sources. I promise, however, that I'll try and never do anything like that again."

Meg stood up and offered her hand to Capobianco. The detective also stood up and stared at the proffered hand in front of her. After a moment's hesitation, she grasped it and shook it. Quietly she said, "Fuck you!" but she had a slight smile on her face.

"Good enough. Capo, Bill, we'll talk soon. I have a feeling that the case against Dr. Davies is about to blow up big and I want you guys to nail his ass to the wall."

She then gave a simple wave to the two of them, turned, and left.

Capobianco sat down and let out a big sigh. She looked at Karb. "Okay, let's think this through. We came into possession of confidential information. We didn't steal it. It was given to us by Meg so it should be admissible. We'll just identify her as a CI. Damn it, I hate when she gets ahead of us."

"Yeah, tell me about it," Karb said. "She's been a pain in my ass for years now. I think we should go to the captain with this. We won't tell him how Meg screwed you over, but we can tell him we got this from her. We're not lawyers. We're going to want someone from the DA's office to read through all of this and see if it's really what Meg says. If it is, we definitely have a motive. If nothing else, it will give us a basis for hauling him into one of the interrogation rooms and applying a bit of pressure. Even if he won't talk, it might shake him up a bit and make him feel like the net is starting to close. What do you think?"

"Yeah, I guess so. I'm going to need a little time before we do that. Give me another moment to process what Meg did and catch my breath."

Karb looked down, and then back up, almost shyly. "That reminds me. My shrink told me I had to socialize with someone."

"And?" Capobianco looked at him with a bemused smile.

"And I was wondering if you might want to go and catch a bite of lunch with me today."

"Oh, my lord, William Russell Karb. Are you asking me out on a date?" Capobianco said this while patting her chest like a Southern belle. He could almost feel the sarcasm drip off her words.

Now it was Karb's turn to have his face flush and he turned and mumbled, "Forget it."

"Bill, that was for you giving me shit when I walked in this morning pissed off about Meg. Of course, I'll go out for lunch. That'll give us some time to work on our pitch to the captain. Where do you want to go?"

"How about The Stepping Stone?"

"That rat trap over on 24th and Quimby? Jesus, Bill, is that the only restaurant you go to? Look, if you're going to take me to lunch, we're going someplace else. Have you ever been to Matt's BBQ?"

"No."

"Good, then I'll get to watch you experience a new restaurant."

"Where is it?" Karb asked.

"As I'll be driving, you don't really need to know that, do you?

Karb stared at her blankly and then just shook his head. "Fine."

"You do like barbecue, don't you?"

Karb shrugged, a completely non-committal response.

"Bill, when was the last time you had barbecue?"

"I don't know," he said with a sense of resignation.

"Jesus, you are *such* a creature of habit. You come to work, you go to the gym, you go home and every week or so you go to The Stepping Stone Cafe. Am I right?"

"How long a drive is it?"

"Don't worry about it, I said I'll drive. We'll leave a bit early and beat the lunch rush. Will that work for you?"

Karb begrudgingly responded "yes" and then turned back to his desk.

Capobianco looked at him for a while, wondering if she might have pushed a bit too far by describing his life in such bleak terms. If she was right about it, and she thought she was, she needed to help Karb expand his horizons and maybe food would be a good place to start.

಄

Karb got home about 7:30 pm. He'd stopped at the gym for a light workout. It had been a while since he'd seen Coach. He'd started on the heavy bag but just felt somewhat listless. At first, he attributed it to fatigue or the barbecue plate he'd devoured for lunch, but then he wondered if maybe it was because he wasn't quite so angry today. He hadn't felt that stress in his shoulders that he so commonly did just before he started beating up the bag.

He grilled up a chicken breast and made a small Caesar salad. He sat in silence as he ate. The only noise in the house was the ticking of the clock on the kitchen wall. After finishing his meal, he rinsed the dishes and put them in the dishwasher. He then stood and stared out his kitchen window. He could see a small group of kids playing basketball just across the street. Absently, he rubbed his bicep without noticing the ridges of scars from his prior efforts at self-soothing.

Sleep did not come easily as the silence of the house seemed particularly deafening. Opening up the drawer to the bedside table, Karb pulled out a safety razor and examined it. He ran it along his left arm, just below the existing scars, but not hard enough to draw blood. This was enough. He stared at the light white line, put the razor back in the drawer, and drifted off to sleep.

Chapter Twenty-Two

"So, first off, did you complete your homework?"

Karb gave a gruff laugh and nodded his head. He wore what Dr. Malone might describe as an awkward smile. She wondered if that was the best he could do. Would she ever be able to get him to the point where he might actually be able to experience joy again? This was not something she would set as a goal for their sessions, but it was her sincere hope.

"Yeah, I went with Capo for some barbecue out on Mississippi."

"And how was it?"

"The food was actually pretty good. I had an order of sliced brisket and Capo had the pork belly burnt ends."

"Bill, I don't care about what you ate. How was it going out with Capo and trying something new?"

"Yeah, I figured that was what you meant." Karb still didn't like talking about himself but had to admit that it had been nice to talk with someone in a casual setting. It reminded him how it had been before Mike Kelley and his family moved to Florida. He had been part of something bigger than himself; he had been part of a family again.

"It was alright. She wouldn't let us talk about our cases, so I mostly listened to her."

"Did you learn anything about her that you didn't know before?"

"Surprisingly, yes. I knew she was divorced but didn't know the details. We also talked about Debbie."

Dr. Malone was pleased that Karb seemed to be able to engage in conversation that didn't involve work. The fact that she had reached out to Capobianco and asked her to not discuss work might have helped.

"How's Debbie doing?"

"It's going to be a slow process. She's out of the hospital and will be in a rehab facility for the next couple of months. We're going up there soon to talk with her. We figure we'll bring her up to date on our cases, just to keep her mind busy. I know if it were me stuck in that bed, I'd be going crazy."

"Bill, I'm proud of you. The fact that you're starting to think about others is really healthy."

"Doc, it wasn't my idea. I only agreed to it when Capo suggested we do it."

"It doesn't matter who came up with the idea, the fact is that you are doing something for someone else. Let me ask you a question, what do you do when you get sad?"

"What do you mean?"

"Everyone gets sad at least every once in a while. I'm sure there are moments when you think about Janice and your son and what your life would be like if they hadn't been murdered."

"Of course."

She could see him starting to tense up and his eyes got slightly hooded.

"Bill, I'm not faulting you for feeling sad. Everyone does and most people don't have nearly as much to be sad about. The question is how you deal with the sadness? How you deal with the grief? There are only a few types of grieving that are unhealthy. You don't seem like the type that drowns their sorrows in a bottle or with drugs."

She looked at him and he shook his head no.

"I know you go to the gym, and I suspect that you use the bags and the sparring to help you. Is that accurate?"

"I guess. I never really thought about it. I just like to go to the gym and break a sweat. Hitting the bags, especially the heavy one, just allows me to…I don't know. It just allows me not to think. I escape…everything, even if only for an hour or so. I almost always feel better when I'm done."

"Does that really work? I mean, when you go home from the gym, do you find yourself in a better mood?"

Karb said nothing and slowly closed his eyes.

"I suspect that the benefit of the gym is that it allows you to avoid the grief. Might that be it?"

She watched him, but he just sat there, with his eyes still closed.

"We sometimes refer to this as deferring grief. You let some steam off when the pressure gets to be too much, but you don't really address the underlying grief. I'm going to ask you a very tough question and I want you to answer truthfully."

Karb didn't move.

"Have you ever tried to hurt yourself?"

Still, Karb sat still with no response.

"Bill?"

She watched him and just let the seconds go by. Slowly, he opened his eyes and looked directly at her. He nodded and softly said, "Yes."

"I would be a little surprised if you hadn't."

A quizzical look came over his face.

"Bill, you've been through more than most and really have never had much of a support network. I understand the Kelley family helped but they weren't there when Janice died and now, they're gone. One of the reasons that I wanted you to go out for lunch is that I want you to develop new relationships. I'm not saying you and Capo have to become best friends, in fact I'd prefer you develop friendships outside of the police force, but your lunch was at least a start.

"The grief will never disappear but as you gain new experiences, especially pleasurable ones, the grief will slowly become a smaller part of your life. You will still experience it and you should. The fact that you miss them so much means you loved them and that's a good thing."

Karb continued to stare into her eyes, and she hoped that he was absorbing at least some of what she was saying.

"Bill, I'm going to give you my card with my cellphone number. I don't do this usually, in fact I've never done it before, but if you ever need to talk, if the grief ever gets so overwhelming that you want to hurt yourself, give me a call."

Karb broke their gaze as he reached out for her business card. Dr. Malone thought she saw a hint of glistening in his eyes, but no tears fell.

Dr. Malone stood first, followed by Karb.

"This was a good session, at least I hope it was for you. When you go up to see Debbie, bring her some decent food. That institutional food must be driving her crazy."

Karb smiled, although tinged with sadness. "Thanks, Doc. See you next week."

Dr. Malone nodded as she watched Karb turn and walk out. She wondered if she could be as strong as him if she had to go through all that he had. She picked up her cellphone and called her husband.

"Hi, Jeff. I just wanted to tell you how much I love you."

❧

Chapter Twenty-Three

*W*elcome to Season Four of *Murder in Bridge City, my podcast for those interested in exploring the violent and ugly underbelly of our fair city of Portland, Oregon. I am your host, Meg Nguyen, and this is Episode Two. I hope all of you are well and avoiding the dark side of our city of roses.*

This season, we've been following a number of particularly inter-esting storylines. Before I go further, I want to bring you up to date on the young woman who was found dead at Lewis & Clark University. The autopsy came back and determined that there was no foul play but, rather, involved an accidental overdose. Out of respect for her family and friends, we are not going to delve into her tragic death any further.

Of the remaining matters we're following, the first involves the bombing of a police vehicle transporting a gangbanger, killing the gang member and a senior detective in charge of the City's gang unit, while also seriously injuring homicide detective Debra Pedersen.

The other storyline involves the suspicious death of Portland socialite Charlene Price Davies. While there have been developments in the bombing case, I'll talk about those next week. This week, I want to share with you an interview with a former co-worker of Charlene

Price Davies' husband, Dr. James Davies. Unlike in prior seasons, I'm not going to summarize the witness' statement but, rather, just let you listen to the interview and allow you to draw your own conclusions.

As soon as we come back from a quick break to thank our sponsors, we'll present the interview of Emad Aboujaoude. Our first sponsor today is…

෯

Welcome back and here is the promised interview with Emad Aboujaoude.

It is June 8th, and my name is Meg Nguyen. I'm talking with Emad Aboujaoude. Emad, can you confirm that I have your consent to record our conversation?

You do.

Okay, Emad, can you give us a little background about yourself?

As you said, my name is Emad Aboujaoude. I was born in Sacramento, California and received my nursing degree from Oregon Health Sciences University. After a couple of years in the ER, I decided that I wanted to work in the OR and became a circulating nurse.

Do you want me to explain what a circulating nurse is?

Yes, please.

While the duties fluctuate somewhat from hospital to hospital, generally a circulating nurse is responsible for the flow of patients and materials into the operating rooms. We make sure that the ORs are fully prepped for the anticipated surgeries.

I really enjoyed my work and had a pretty good rapport with most of the surgeons and the surgical staff. We work with the patients before the surgery and then, when the procedure begins, we assist the surgeon by handing him or her the necessary surgical instruments.

Is that where you met Dr. J. Matthew Davies?

[audible sigh]

Yes, actually I worked on multiple operations where he was the anesthesiologist. I wouldn't say that we had much of a relationship, other than a completely professional one. Dr. Davies didn't seem interested in talking to anyone who wasn't an MD, unless absolutely necessary. Some doctors are like that. I don't know if it is the God complex, or they just think their education automatically makes them better than everyone else. Dr. Davies was one of those. It just seemed like he was quietly, but obviously, arrogant.

Okay, was there a particular surgery that had an impact upon you?

Yes, a patient was getting a quadruple bypass. This is a very technical procedure, although not an uncommon operation. The patient was relatively young…if I recall correctly, he was in his early to mid-forties.

In any event, the procedure is to put the patient on a heart-lung bypass machine that circulates his blood from outside of the patient's body and allows the surgeon to work on the heart. The heart actually stops beating during the time the patient is on the bypass machine. Once the arteries are reattached, the surgeon often applies a small electric shock to get the heart pumping again. Some surgeons prefer that the anesthesiologist inject adrenaline to give the heart a little boost.

Once the heart is beating again, they check for any leaks or obvious weaknesses to the heart and arteries and then sew the patient back up. That is a very basic description of a very complex procedure.

What was unusual about this particular procedure?

Well, it is common for me to move around the OR as necessary. While the patient was still on bypass, I was walking behind Dr. Davies and saw him pull a small vial out of the top shelf of his cart.

Emad, can you explain what you mean by a cart?

Oh, sure, well things are much different these days. Over the past several years, just about every major hospital uses a computerized medication dispenser in the OR. The anesthesiologist will code in the patient's name and as he takes out various medications, the computer inputs those medications in the patient's chart.

Back then, it was more common for an anesthesiologist to have a simple cart with all of his medications. He would make handwritten notes about which medications he gave the patient.

Can you describe what the cart looked like?

This is going to sound odd, but it was essentially a tool cart, like the ones you can get a Sears or at a Napa store. In fact, the most popular cart was a Craftsman tool cart with multiple drawers. They were less expensive than the carts manufactured by the medical supply companies and just as good. I remember that Dr. Davies had a red Craftsman cart with chrome edges and five different drawers.

Okay, I get it. So, did something unusual happen?

Well, the surgeon was just completing the procedure and was getting ready to take the patient off of the heart-lung bypass. I was walking by Dr. Davies when I saw him reach into the top drawer of his cart and remove a small vial. He then injected it into the patient's IV.

Was this anything unusual?

No, not at all. The anesthesiologist is constantly monitoring the patient and injecting various medications into the IV throughout the course of the surgery. He needs to make sure that the general anesthetic is at an appropriate level and that the patient's vitals are constant.

So why did you consider Dr. Davies injecting this vial to be unusual? Did you see what the vial was?

Well, not right away. I assumed it was an antiplatelet to help prevent blood clots or Naloxone which is used to help the patient start coming out of general anesthesia.

Out of just natural curiosity, I asked him what he was giving the patient. I could see his face immediately get flushed, even behind his mask, and he told me to mind my own business.

Do you remember exactly what he said?

I do as he practically spat out the words. He said, "Nurse, do your job and leave me to mine." I felt like I had been slapped.

Did you happen to see the label on the vial?

I wish I could say that I did. The vials are pretty small, and the labels are even smaller with tiny printing. I did notice, however, that the largest print on the label was longer than I would have expected for either the common names for the antiplatelet or Naloxone.

I was a little shaken by Dr. Davies' verbal attack so kept my distance after that.

What happened then?

Well, the patient was taken off the heart-lung machine and the surgeon released the clamp on the aorta. Normally, the heart will start beating almost immediately but this time it didn't. The surgeon then tried a mild electrical charge which, as I said, is also common. Still, the heart didn't start up.

He then ordered Dr. Davies to inject adrenaline into the heart and tried another electrical charge.

This went on for ten minutes with the surgeon manually pumping the heart while they tried to get it going. After ten minutes, he called it. The patient was dead.

That must have been quite a shock for you.

Anytime a patient dies in the OR, it is a shock. We are all aware of the risks and the surgeons always explain them to the patient and the family. Nonetheless, death is pretty rare, even for a quadruple bypass like this.

What was Dr. Davies doing at this time?

Quite honestly, I couldn't tell you. Everyone was focusing on the patient, and I was alert in case I was asked to do something. In situations like that, there is no time to be distracted or to hesitate when a patient is coding.

Once the patient is declared dead, it is like a balloon has just burst. Everyone is in shock and staring at each other. I remember looking at Dr. Davies at that time and he was staring at me. I almost felt like he was accusing me of somehow being responsible.

As I started to get back to work, I saw him walk out of the OR.

I looked around to see if anyone was watching me and then walked over to the medication cart. I opened the top drawer just to see if I could figure out what that last injection was. You need to understand that the various vials come in packs of twelve or more and are kept in the bottom half of the box with the top torn off for ease when grabbing them.

I noticed that one of the boxes had a single vial missing. I looked at the label on the box and it was for potassium chloride.

I'm sorry, what is potassium chloride?

It is a very common drug used as a muscle relaxant.

Is it used in heart surgery?

Absolutely not. The heart is a muscle and when you are trying to restart a heart after bypass surgery, the last thing you want is for the heart to be relaxed. A full dose would actually prevent the heart from restarting.

Could you see what happened to the actual vial he used? Could you confirm whether or not it was potassium chloride?

No, immediately after a vial or needle is used, it is placed in a sharp's container, and I can't see it.

But you suspected that Dr. Davies might have injected potassium chloride into the patient?

I did.

And you suspected that that drug might have prevented the heart from restarting and killed the patient?

I did.

Well, what did you do about this suspicion?

Nothing.

Nothing? You didn't tell anyone? You didn't report this?

Meg, you need to understand the realities of hospitals, especially back then. I had two strikes against me if I were to even consider reporting my suspicions. First, I am a male nurse. I can't tell you how many doctors still think of nursing as a woman's job and assume that a male nurse is either a failed medical student or gay or both.

Secondly, and I suspect you can relate to this, as a person of color, my credibility is always questioned. I'll admit it is getting better as more minorities become doctors and nurses but back when this happened, the Oregon medical community was still overwhelmingly male and white.

I did have some vague conversations with my supervisor, as well as a couple of friends who were younger surgeons. They all told me that unless I was one hundred percent certain and willing to risk my career, I had better keep my suspicions to myself.

So, what did you do?

I protected my career. I had two young kids at the time and couldn't afford to lose my job. I also left Good Sam and went to work at Portland Adventist. I wanted to make sure that I never had to deal with Dr. Davies again.

Wouldn't the potassium chloride show up in an autopsy?

If there was an autopsy, maybe, but they generally wouldn't have checked for that. They'd look for narcotics mostly. In this case, however, the assumption was that the heart was too damaged and couldn't stand the strain of the bypass surgery. As far as I know, no autopsy was ever ordered.

Emad, I want to thank you for your candor. Before we wrap this up, do you happen to know the name of the patient that died that day?

Absolutely, his name was Ken Price. I heard that he had been an exec at Nike and had a wife and daughter. I always felt bad about not at least reaching out to them. It still bothers me to this day.

CHAPTER TWENTY-FOUR

"So, how are you doing?"

Davies looked up from the menu. He glanced around at the other tables and responded quietly, "Yeah, I don't really know. I'm nervous and not sure what's going to happen next and how this is going to work out."

"That's why I'm here, Jim. After we finish our meal, we're going to head back to my office and meet up with Bahij Jada."

"The guy at your firm?"

"Yes," Randy responded. "Bahij is in charge of the firm's criminal practice. Mostly this involves white collar crime, but he spent enough time in the DA's office and the US Attorney's office when he was younger that he should be able to help us. I explained the basics to him and made a personal request that he represent you."

"Am I going to be arrested?"

"Jim, Bahij is as good as they come. He'll be able to tell you better, but I just can't imagine that the police will have enough evidence that would support charging you. Let's not worry about that right now. Did you call your hospitals and clinics and tell them you needed a leave of absence?"

"I did. There's no problem there. Especially after the pissant nurse gave the interview to the podcaster, hell, they want me to take off as much time as I need, if not more. I'm concerned that they are all going to revoke my privileges. Randy, I need some money. I want to avoid cashing in my investment accounts. Are you sure we can't get some money from the trust? I am the main beneficiary now, aren't I?"

"Look, Jim, I want to be careful about getting you money from the trust while all of this crap with the police is going on. If you need me to, I will float you some money until the dust settles."

The waiter approached the table and asked, "Gentlemen, have you decided what you'd like for lunch?"

Randy spoke first, "I'll go with a caprese salad and the scallops."

"Very good, sir." The waiter turned to Dr. Davies. "And for you, sir?"

Davies stared at the menu. The University Club of Portland had a wonderful, and very private, dining room but the menu seemed to be too much for him to comprehend.

"My friend will have the BLT sandwich with fresh fruit," Wilkerson ordered.

"Of course, gentlemen. May I get you another drink?"

"Yes, I'll have another Manhattan…no, let's switch over to ice teas for both of us. We need to make sure that we keep our heads clear."

"Yes, sir. I'll bring those right over."

Wilkerson looked over at Davies who was still staring at the menu. He gently reached for the menu and took it out of Davies' hands.

"Jim? Jim?"

Davies looked up and at his old friend.

"Jim, everything is going to be fine. We've walked through this before, but I'll do so again. It's going to be uncomfortable for a while. The police are going to do their investigation but, at the end of the day, they'll have nothing. As long as you are careful with what you say, they can't do much. They may be able to come up with a motive but they won't be able to prove that you pushed Char down the stairs. Without that proof, they're unlikely to even bother charging you. You just need to remember that you can't talk to anyone, only me and Bahij."

"Have you spoken with Kelly yet?"

"Yes, I met with her the other day. She'll be at the memorial."

"Did she mention when she is coming down?"

Wilkerson reached over and placed his hand on his friend's forearm resting on the table. "Jim, she's already here. I put her up at the Nines.

"If she contacts you, which I assume she won't, don't talk to her any more than is absolutely necessary. I'll deal with her. I don't want her stirring things up at all. I know you two weren't close but if she suspects that you had something to do with Char's death, it could cause problems."

Davies placed his hand over his friend's. "What about that podcaster? Did you hear her podcast yesterday? Isn't that going to be a problem?"

"Jim, there's nothing we can do about public opinion. Anyway, since when do you care what anyone thinks? I'm not worried about Meg Nguyen. As long as we keep our eye on the police investigation, she can't do anything that will hurt you.

"You need to take a deep breath and just stay calm. As long as you just talk to Bahij and me, and no one else, you'll be fine. Also, Jim, even if you do lose your privileges, it'll be alright. You're about to be a very rich man soon. You trust me, right?"

Davies nodded his head up and down. Wilkerson pulled his hand back from Davies' arm as the waiter brought their ice teas.

CHAPTER TWENTY-FIVE

arb put down the receiver. "The captain wants to see us."

"Shit. It's about Meg's podcast, isn't it?"

"Capo, I don't know but probably. Nothing that the nurse said is going to help our case but it's definitely going to turn the heat up on us to come up with something. We're making some progress. Hopefully, he'll be happy with that."

"When have you ever known the captain to be happy?"

"Fair point." Karb stood up and quickly put on his jacket. "Let's go."

On the walk to the captain's office, Karb almost felt as if he was walking the plank. He hadn't really spoken with the captain in the last week or so and wasn't sure how much he knew about his progress with his therapist. It was going to take a while for him to reestablish his relationship with the captain, but he just wasn't sure how much time he had to do that.

Karb knocked on the door and they both heard a voice bark, "Come in."

The captain was, as always, impeccably attired in his standard uniform—a three-piece suit, this one pin-striped, a white shirt, a subtly printed tie, and black wingtip shoes. Karb thought he looked more tired than usual. The stress that came with the job could be considerable and Captain Schnadig had been doing this for seven years. Karb wondered which of them would still be here five years from now. If he had been a betting man, the odds would be pretty even, at least from looking at the exhaustion on the captain's face.

"I'm getting phone calls from both the chief and the mayor. Walk me through what you have."

Capobianco started, "Well, Captain, first let me say that Meg's recent interview isn't really helpful…"

"Detective, I don't care about that podcast. The fact that Davies may have killed his wife's first husband is interesting, in a sordid, tabloid sort of way, but obviously doesn't prove that he killed his wife. Let's not waste time talking about Nguyen's muckraking."

"Yes, sir," Capobianco responded, and then she proceeded to lay out the relevant facts so far. "We know that Davies took out a new life insurance policy on his wife three months ago. This is unusual as she is worth somewhere between twenty-five and fifty million dollars, depending on the stock market."

"How much is the life insurance for?" the captain interjected.

"Three million dollars."

The captain nodded his head and motioned for her to continue.

"The vic's money is in a trust set up by her first husband. The lawyer who drafted it is Randy Wilkerson, who also appears to be longtime friends with Davies. Apparently, they went to college together. The trust agreement is unusual in that it permitted the vic to change its terms if she wanted to."

"Why is that unusual?"

"I spoke with a lawyer who specializes in estate planning and high value trusts. Given the situation, it is most common for a family trust to become at least partially irrevocable once the first of the initial grantors dies."

"Detective, break that down. I'm not a lawyer."

"Absolutely, sir, and neither am I. The attorney explained that the general practice is to protect the couple's children when the first of them dies by preventing the survivor from changing the trust, or at least a portion of the trust. He explained that the concern is always that the surviving spouse might remarry and cut the children of the first marriage out of the trust. The term he used was gold-digger. A wealthy spouse will want to ensure that any gold-digger can't take advantage of the surviving spouse to screw the children out of their inheritance."

"And in this case, how many children were there?"

"Just a single child. Her name is Kelly Price, and she lives in Seattle. From what we've gathered so far, she was somewhat estranged from her mom and didn't get along at all with the stepdad, Davies."

"Okay, so this trust was a standard trust. Did the vic change it?"

"She did. Apparently about a week or so before she died, she changed the trust so that if she died, the primary beneficiary becomes Davies, and the daughter only gets a small monthly stipend. When Davies dies, the daughter then gets the balance of the trust, assuming that Davies hasn't burned through the whole thing."

The captain closed his eyes, looked down, and started rubbing his temples with both hands.

"Let me see if I've got this straight. Randy Wilkerson set up a trust for Ken and Charlene Price. For some reason, he doesn't draft a standard trust agreement but, instead, sets it up to allow the survivor of Ken and Charlene Price to amend the trust. Then after Ken Price dies, Charlene marries Wilkerson's longtime friend and a week before she dies, she amends the trust to benefit Dr. Davies. In addition, Dr. Davies took out a large life insurance policy on his wife."

"Yes, sir, that's all correct." This was Karb who spoke, and the captain lifted his head and stared at him. "It is also important to note that Charlene, had she survived, could have changed the trust again to cut him out entirely. This would seem to be a motive for him to kill her before she could do so."

"So, are Dr. Davies and Wilkerson in cahoots?"

"Captain, not that we've been able to establish. Wilkerson is a big fish in the legal community, and it wouldn't make sense for him to risk his reputation just to help his friend."

"And how do you propose we find out?"

Capobianco answered, "Bill had an idea and I'm not sure how I feel about it."

"Go on."

"So, the communications between Wilkerson and the vic are still protected by the attorney-client privilege, as are any communications between Wilkerson and Dr. Davies. Without access to Wilkerson's file and any notes and emails, we don't know what he did or didn't tell Charlene about amending the trust.

"Bill suggested that we talk to the daughter and gently hint that Wilkerson might have committed malpractice. The attorney I spoke with about this whole trust stuff confirmed that Kelly Price likely has a claim against Wilkerson to the extent that he drafted something outside of the norm that ended up depriving her of her inheritance."

"Go on." The captain's eyes showed significant interest.

"As part of a malpractice claim, her lawyer might be able to force Wilkerson to release his files."

"And we'd be able to see those files?"

"Maybe. The attorney told me that Wilkerson might seek some sort of protective order from the Court that would limit disclosure of his confidential communications with Ken Price, Charlene Price Davies, and James Davies. It will be up to the Court whether or not to allow disclosure to the daughter's attorney. Given that both Ken Price and Charlene are dead, there might be an argument that there is no compelling reason to retain the confidentiality. Anyway, we thought it might be worth a shot."

The captain turned his chair so that he could look out the window. It was another cloudy day in downtown Portland, but the clouds seemed to momentarily part and the captain could see a patch of blue sky.

"I like it. Detectives, I want you to have a talk with the daughter. Be very diplomatic. I don't want her saying that the police suggested that she pursue a malpractice claim. You can inquire but not suggest. Do you understand?"

"Captain," Karb spoke up, "I was planning on talking to the daughter."

The captain turned to Karb and took a long and deep breath. "No, Bill. I get that it was your idea but if this comes back to you, the whole investigation could blow up. You're still toxic in the DA's office, as well as City Hall. We'll let Capo have the talk with the girl."

Karb fought the urge to clench his fists and argue. Instead, he could feel the muscles in his upper arms and shoulders tighten but refused to let his reaction show on his face.

"Yes, sir," was all he said.

"Okay, anything else?"

"No sir," Karb responded, and the captain knew he was upset and trying to maintain control. He had seen him explode in the past. Karb maintaining his composure was a good sign.

Karb continued, "We might have a couple of other things to look into but not worth bothering you about yet."

"Okay, good work. Oh, by the way, do I want to know how you know what the trust agreement says?"

Capobianco looked first at Karb and then back to the captain. "No, sir, let's just say it was a confidential source."

The captain took another deep breath and let out an audible sigh. He turned to a file on his desk, looked down, and waved his hand for them to leave.

Chapter Twenty-Six

"Dr. Davies, would you like something to drink?"

"Thank you, LaVonne. Can I have some Perrier?"

"Of course, sir, I'll be right back."

"So, Jim, Bahij will be here in a couple of minutes."

"And you're sure he's the best guy to represent me?"

"Absolutely, he's a heavy hitter. The fact that he hasn't handled any capital murder cases in decades will tell the police that you are concerned enough to retain an attorney but not so concerned to hire a capital murder lawyer. We're sending just the right message."

"Okay, Randy. You know I trust you."

"As well you should."

Just then, the door opened and Bahij Jada strode in. Jada wasn't tall, but he had an athlete's physique that his tailored suit accentuated. He was balding, with dark skin and his glasses perched midway down the bridge of his aquiline nose. His eyes were intense, and Dr. Davies found himself instantly mesmerized by them.

Bahij Jada knew the effect his looks had on people, and he always used them to his best advantage. His intensity intimidated most people but, fortunately, not his wife or children.

"Dr. Davies," he began, reaching out to shake Davies' hand, "I'm Bahij. It's a pleasure to meet you."

"Thank you, Mr. Jada."

"Nope, if I'm going to be your attorney, we have to be on a first name basis. Please call me Bahij. May I call you Jim or do you prefer James?"

Davies was used to dealing with egotistical and overbearing surgeons but had never met anyone that exuded such a complete presence that seemed to fill up the entire room.

"Um, Jim will be fine."

"Great," Jada said as he sat down across from Davies and Wilkerson. He pulled a black fountain pen and started writing immediately.

"Now, it is my understanding that you are going to place a ten-thousand-dollar retainer in our trust account and that you've already signed our retainer agreement."

Wilkerson spoke up, "Bahij, the family trust has placed the retainer in our trust account."

Jada frowned at that but chose to address it with Wilkerson at a later time.

"Okay, now that we've established an attorney-client relationship, let me lay down the ground rules. You will never lie to me."

"Of course," Davies said, a slight note of annoyance in his voice.

"No, I want to make sure you understand what I am saying. You can lie to your friends, you can even lie to your priest, but you can never *ever* lie to me. I need to know everything, both the good and the bad, although especially the bad. I rely upon what you tell me and what our investigator discovers. I will then develop our strategy based upon the information I have. If there are pertinent facts that I don't know about, I can't plan for them, and if I can't plan for them, they can unravel our entire strategy. In other words, what I don't know can hurt you…a lot. Is that clear?"

"Yes."

"Good, now there are some things that I might not ask you and that is because I have certain ethical obligations. For example, if you were to tell me that you, in fact, killed your wife, I would then be prohibited from telling the police or a judge or a jury that you didn't. If that were to happen, I would need to resign as your attorney and the inferences that might be drawn from such a resignation could be very damaging to you."

He continued, "I'm not trying to split hairs and I'm absolutely not suggesting that you killed your wife, but we need to be very clear about this. I'm going to be asking you certain questions and I want you to answer those questions truthfully and fully. What I don't want is for you to give me answers to questions that I haven't asked.

"For example, if I ask if you know the time, I don't want you to tell me," Jada paused and looked at his watch, "that it is 2:15 pm. The reason I don't want you to tell me is because that isn't the answer to my question. The question was whether or not you know what time it is. The answer to *that* question is either yes or no. If I then ask you to tell me what time it is, you can then do so. If I don't ask you that follow up question, I don't want you telling me.

"It's all about not educating the other side. Do you understand?"

Davies looked at Wilkerson and then back at Jada. He was not used to being spoken to like this and could feel his aggravation start to grow. This attorney was being condescending and that was something Davies had been accused of but never tolerated from others. Before he could speak, however, Wilkerson put his hand on Davies' arm and leaned in.

"Jim, Bahij is doing his job. He needs to lay down these ground rules in order to best represent you and protect you. He doesn't think you've done anything wrong, but this is just the way it's done."

Jada leaned back in his chair and clasped his hands across his chest. He was good at reading people and saw that this client had a short fuse and was not used to following someone else's lead.

"Jim, if I've offended you, I apologize. The rules I've laid down are important and the only way that I can represent you completely and competently. I realize that this may be a bit awkward for a while as we're talking about the death of your wife but I'm confident that you'll get used to it quickly. Should we proceed, or would you prefer to retain an alternate attorney?"

Davies fought through his indignation and nodded his head.

"Okay, I want you to walk me through everything that happened the day *before* you found your wife's body. Let's start with this. First of all, where do you work?"

"I work for a number of smaller hospitals outside of the metropolitan area, as well as a couple of private surgical centers throughout the city."

Jada stared at him for a moment and then said, "Is there a reason you don't work at the local hospitals? Is that your decision or the hospitals'?"

Davies responded, almost spitting, "It was my decision! I'm old-fashioned and don't like the automation that the major hospital providers have adopted. Everything is done electronically, from recording the various drugs I use to actually dispensing them. I prefer to do things the way I was trained to do and that doesn't involve typing everything into a computer."

"Okay, I can understand that," Jada said, holding up his pen and yellow legal pad.

"So, walk me through the day before your wife passed. Did you work that day?"

The two men then slowly and painstakingly went through Dr. Davies' full day from breakfast to dinner and going to bed. This process took more than an hour with Jada constantly writing notes on his legal pad, rarely looking up when he asked a follow up question.

The same process was followed for the next day, although Jada was very careful as to how he posed his questions. He asked a series of questions about what happened without having to ask his client whether he had, in fact, murdered his wife.

The entire meeting took over three hours, interrupted only by repeated requests from Dr. Davies for additional bottles of Perrier.

Chapter Twenty-Seven

Karb walked up to the neighbors' house. He would describe it as a traditional-looking house, probably colonial or something like that. It was the type of house he might expect to see in New England or along the East Coast, even though he'd never been there. It was a light gray with four pillars spanning the front porch. In the driveway, he noticed a dark Volvo station wagon parked up close to the garage door. The grass was freshly mowed and there were flowering baskets on either side of the porch.

He looked carefully before walking up the stairs towards the front door and confirmed that there was a Ring camera doorbell. Under his breath he muttered, "Come on, I need something here."

As he took the first of the four concrete steps, he heard a voice from around the side of the house.

"Can I help you with something?"

He saw a middle-aged woman with curly red hair. She was wearing worn jeans with rubber rain boots and a flannel shirt. "Mrs. Hollenbeck?"

"Yes?" He noticed that her voice had a slightly higher pitch as she answered and her grip on the rake she was holding tightened.

"I'm Detective Bill Karb with the Portland Police Department."

"Yes?" Her voice lowered slightly. He could always tell when the tone of a simple response changed from fear of possible physical harm to fear of the unknown. She walked up on to the porch, moving toward the front door.

"Well, I'm doing an investigation of Mrs. Davies' death and was wondering if I could…"

"Oh, that poor woman. We've been neighbors for over five years or so, and she was just the sweetest person."

Karb could tell this woman felt genuine affection for her late neighbor, something that wasn't nearly as common these days as it once was.

"Do you think she was murdered?" she asked, her voice slightly lowered and with an almost conspiratorial tone.

"Ma'am, we're just doing a general investigation at this point. It is our standard procedure to confirm how someone passed."

The woman nodded as if in agreement.

"I notice that you have a Ring camera doorbell."

"We do, my husband had it installed just a couple of months ago."

"I was wondering if I might access your account and check the video."

"Detective, if I had any idea how to do that, I would certainly allow you to."

Karb gave her a warm smile. "Thank you, Ma'am. May I come over and hand you my card?"

"Of course, can I offer you something cold to drink? It's starting to get a bit warm out here."

"Thank you, Ma'am, but I need to contact some of your other neighbors."

Karb walked up the rest of the concrete steps and met the woman in front of the porch. He handed her his business card which she promptly examined with great care.

"The next step is for me to contact something called the Neighbors Public Safety Service and request to view your videos.

They will contact you and ask if I may have access. I just wanted to introduce myself in advance and make the request personally rather than you just getting some random email."

Mrs. Hollenbeck smiled and said, "That is very thoughtful, Detective. I will look out for your email. What other neighbors are you planning on talking to?"

"Likely the ones on either side of your house. Do you know them?"

"The Browns live over there," she said, pointing to a white Colonial house, "and the Andersons live over there." She pointed to a slightly smaller brick home. "Neither of them is home right now, but I can either give you their phone numbers or ask them to call you. Which would you prefer?"

"The phone numbers would be great. I've sometimes found that people are often willing to talk to the police but won't always initiate a contact."

Mrs. Hollenbeck gave a knowing smile and reached for her phone. She gave Karb the telephone numbers for her neighbors.

"Are you sure you don't want a glass of water or perhaps some iced tea?"

"Thank you, Ma'am, but I really need to get back to the office and place my request with Ring. You may get an email as early as the end of the day."

"Will you let me know if you see anything?"

"I'm sorry, ma'am, but I can't. We have to maintain a certain confidentiality when investigating possible crimes. I do appreciate your cooperation and, of course, the offer of something to drink."

The woman smiled at the detective and Karb nodded his head in response before turning away and walking back to his car. As he settled behind the wheel, he watched as she pulled her cell-phone out of her pocket and dialed a number. Karb was always impressed, but not surprised, by how quickly a neighborhood grapevine operates. It didn't matter if it was a rundown apartment complex or an upscale area like this, people gossip.

෨

Chapter Twenty-Eight

Meg watched the front door as she took a long sip of her beer. While she generally preferred a nice bourbon, a cool beer on a warm day always seemed to slake her thirst. Joyce sat beside her, sipping on a white wine.

"Do you think she'll really show up?"

"Joyce, she was so helpful when I was at Wilkerson's office, it was almost like she was starstruck. Apparently, some people are impressed by my celebrity!"

Both of them laughed and Joyce reminded her, "Just don't let that head of yours get too big. We need a break in this case if we're going to make it…"

Meg put her hand on Joyce's forearm and said, "There she is!"

They both noticed a middle-aged Black woman walk through the door and squint in the darkness of the bar. The Swine Moonshine + Whiskey Bar was on the ground floor of the Paramount Hotel. The ground floor was actually split in two—a restaurant on one side of the building and the bar located on the other. The bar was known for farm-to-fork pub food with an impressive selection of whiskeys.

Meg raised her hand to get the woman's attention. They locked eyes and LaVonne Floyd walked over.

"Mrs. Floyd, this is my producer, Joyce McCarthy."

Mrs. Floyd sat down across from the two and reached out to shake their hands. "Please call me LaVonne."

"LaVonne, it is a pleasure to meet you. Meg told me how helpful you were when she was in the office."

Mrs. Floyd laughed, her voice both soft and throaty. "You can't imagine how angry Mr. Wilkerson was after you left. I thought he was going to fire me, but he was talked out of it when one of the other partners pointed out that it was the receptionist, and not me, who actually introduced her as the police detective. Meg, I've got to tell you, I've met a lot of ballsy people over the years, but you take the cake. Impersonating a police officer? Isn't that a crime?"

"Now, LaVonne, I never said I was a police officer. The receptionist made an assumption and I just played along."

Mrs. Floyd laughed again and gave Meg a genuine smile. "I'll say it again, you've got balls, girl!"

When the waiter came by, Mrs. Floyd ordered a Bulleit bourbon on the rocks and Meg and Joyce nodded for another round for themselves.

As the waiter walked away, Joyce spoke first, "LaVonne, may I ask how long you've worked for Randy Wilkerson?"

Shaking her head, she responded, "It was fifteen years last May. Do you want to know what he gave me for this anniversary of working together?"

Both Joyce and Meg nodded.

"Nothing! The putz didn't even remember. I got a gift card to the Ringside from the firm but not even an acknowledgement from him."

The bitterness in her voice was obvious and probably explained why she had been willing to give a copy of the trust documents to Meg.

Joyce continued, "We're trying to get a little more background on him."

"What," Mrs. Floyd responded, "you want to know more about the Silver Fox than you can get from the *Portland Magazine* or the other local rags?"

Joyce continued, "Yeah, we know that he's never been married but we can't even find out who he's been dating. Has he ever been in a long-term relationship?"

"If by relationship you mean friendship, he and Dr. Davies have been friends all the way back to college. Other than that, he was more known for dalliances than any sort of relationship of substance. If I had to guess, I'd say his ego won't find anyone good enough because they'll never love him as much as he loves himself, the narcissistic little prick! I'm sorry, I shouldn't have said that. It's just been a long week."

"Don't worry about it," Meg said, "this will stay between the three of us."

The waiter came by and placed their drinks in front of each of them. Mrs. Floyd took a slow but deep draw on her bourbon and let out an audible sigh as she placed the glass back down on the table.

"That bad, huh?"

"Maybe it's just that I'm getting old and have less tolerance for his ego. I do need to correct myself, though. In all the years I've worked for him, he'd never had what I would consider a serious adult relationship until the last year or so. It actually seemed as if someone had been able to break through the veneer and actually hook him."

"Really?" Both Meg and Joyce leaned forward slightly.

"Who was it?" Joyce asked.

"That's the weird thing. I mean he's always been pretty private, at least around me, but he was almost paranoid with this woman and maintained utmost privacy. She only called him on his cellphone, so I never spoke with her. When she would call, or if he called her, he always closed his door and spoke softly so I couldn't hear. I know better than to pry, but I couldn't help but notice that he acted so differently than he had with any other woman I'd known him to be with. After talking to her, I'd swear he even had a little skip to his step. You'd think the man had never been in love before."

"Is it still going on?"

"That's the thing. I think the woman broke it off. A few months ago, Mr. Wilkerson had me make a reservation at this really fancy restaurant in McMinnville. I had to look it up. This place is really bougee. It's the type of place I'd never go to, but Mr. Wilkerson always seems to know the places to go to impress."

"Do you remember the name?"

"It was called ōkta. It has a funny spelling."

"Do you remember when this was?"

"Absolutely, it was the last Saturday in March. I've got to tell you though, however he thought this might impress the woman, apparently it didn't."

"Why do you say that?"

"When he came in that Monday morning, well, let's just say that he was in a mood. Dr. Davies came by and, even with the door closed, I could hear a little and apparently the woman broke up with him. For someone like Randy Wilkerson, no one breaks up with him. When I overheard that, I had to laugh just a little. I know that sounds mean but the guy just, well sometimes people need to experience heartbreak. I figured it might be good for him.

"If it has, however, I haven't noticed any improvement yet. He's still as self-centered as ever."

The women continued to talk for another thirty minutes before Mrs. Floyd said that she had to catch her bus and get home to her family. Before leaving, however, she said to both Meg and Joyce, "Please make sure you keep my name out of the podcast. While I love listening to it, any mention of me would cost me my job and I just can't afford that. Is that alright?"

"No one is accusing you of turning over the trust documents?" Meg asked.

"No, I was pretty good about that. It's driving them crazy, but they haven't really looked at me yet. Can you make sure that they don't?"

Meg answered, "I printed out all of the documents and then scanned them into a new memory stick. That way, there's no metadata that they can trace back to you or even the firm."

"Thank you, that will help me sleep a bit better."

Meg reached out and grasped her hands. "LaVonne, I promise that you'll remain in the background. We'll never say anything or do anything that might cost you your job. I promise."

"Thank you." Mrs. Floyd stood up. "Meg it was nice to see you again, this time as the real you. Joyce, it was nice to meet you as well."

After completing their goodbyes, Mrs. Floyd left the bar, and the two women watched her as she walked out the door and down the sidewalk towards the bus stop.

"Okay," Joyce said, "how are we going to find out who the mystery woman is?"

"I'll drive out to the restaurant and talk to the staff. Someone might have recognized her and know something. Who would have thought that someone would hook the Silver Fox and then let him go?"

They finished their drinks and settled up their tab. Walking out the door, Joyce turned to Meg and simply said, "I've got an odd feeling about this."

"I hate to say I told you so, but I said that there was something to this story."

Joyce hooked her arm around Meg's as they walked up the street to their car.

CHAPTER TWENTY-NINE

"Good afternoon, Bill. What are you looking at?"

"I got the access to the neighbor's Ring recordings for the night Charlene Davies died."

Capobianco sat down at her desk and promptly spilled her coffee on to her lap. As she righted the cup and quickly stood up, she yelled, "Jesus Christ! Bill, get me some paper towels."

Karb stared at her as she was frantically trying to wipe the hot, dark liquid off of her pants. For the first time in longer than he could remember, Karb started laughing. It was a deep and loud laugh, causing everyone else in the room to turn.

"Fuck you, Bill. Get me some goddamn paper towels."

Karb, however, couldn't stop laughing and continued to sit and revel in Capobianco's misery. Capobianco looked and realized that Karb was having too good of a time to be of any assistance, so she turned and walked towards the restroom.

By the time she returned, Karb was just finishing cleaning up the spill on her desk and the floor below. He smirked but didn't say a thing as he sat back down to watch more video.

"Bill, you can really be a dick sometimes. I don't appreciate…"

She stopped as Karb raised his hand to silence her. She had seen the look on his face a couple of times through the years. It was a look that told her that he'd found something important.

"What is it?"

"Do me a favor, run a quick DMV search on a light-colored Bentley Continental, it looks like the license plate is S-H-A-R-K-1."

"Of course, but what is going on? What did you find?"

"Capo, just run the search and then I'll let you know."

As Capobianco logged on to the website for the Oregon Department of Motor Vehicles, Karb called up Officer Sprehe's police report, as well as the coroner's report.

"Bill, the car is listed to Randy Wilkerson. What did you find?"

Standing up and putting on his jacket, Karb said, "Capo, I'll fill you in on the way. Let's go talk to the captain."

~

CHAPTER THIRTY

*W*elcome to Season Four of Murder in Bridge City, *my podcast for those interested in exploring the violent and ugly underbelly of our fair city of Portland, Oregon. I am your host, Meg Nguyen, and this is Episode Three. I hope all of you are well and avoiding the dark side of our city of roses.*

This season, we've been following two particularly interesting storylines. The first involves the bombing of a police vehicle transporting a gangbanger, killing the gang member and a senior detective in charge of the City's gang unit, while also seriously injuring homicide detective Debra Pedersen. While I promise I'll fill you in on the recent developments in that case in a minute, I really want to talk about our other main storyline.

As you will recall, we've been investigating the suspicious death of Portland socialite Charlene Price Davies. By way of background, Charlene was married to an early Nike executive who died, under curious circumstances, during a routine heart bypass operation. In last week's episode, you heard my interview with Emad Aboujaoude, a circulating nurse who was present during the operation and suspects that the patient, Ken Price, may have been killed by the anesthesiologist, Dr. James Matthew Davies.

Too much time has passed and with only the suspicions of Mr. Aboujaoude, Dr. Davies was never even questioned about this possible murder.

Dr. Davies, however, is a close friend of Portland's tax and estate planning lawyer to the local rich and wealthy, Randy Wilkerson. If you recognize the name, it's because he has long been called Portland's most eligible bachelor. In addition to being friends with Dr. Davies, Randy Wilkerson was also good friends with, and the lawyer for, Ken Price and his then-wife, then widow, Charlene.

"Meg, slow down! You're way too excited and throwing too many facts out too quickly. The listeners won't be able to follow the story."

"Yeah, I know, Joyce, but this has just gotten so…I don't even know how to describe it."

"Hey, I get it," Joyce said, reaching over and giving Meg's hand a light squeeze. "Let's take a quick break and rework the script. How much coffee have you had today?"

Meg smiled and lowered her gaze. "Probably too much."

"Okay, let's work on the script and have you drink some water."

"How about a shot of tequila?"

"Meg!"

"No really, it will calm me down. Just one?"

"Alright, but just one and then we focus on the rewrite."

"Care to join me…for just one?"

Joyce laughed as Meg poured two shot glasses and handed one to her. Raising her glass up high, Meg said, "Here's to our breakout episode of the season!"

The two women clinked glasses and drank their shots with a flourish. An hour and a half later, and with half a bottle of tequila gone, they were ready to try again with Meg speaking at a more relaxed pace.

Welcome back to Episode Three of Season Four of Murder in Bridge City, *my podcast for those interested in exploring the violent and ugly underbelly of our fair city of Portland, Oregon. I am your host, Meg Nguyen, and I hope all of you are well and avoiding the dark side of our city of roses.*

This season, we've been following two particularly interesting storylines. The first involves the bombing of a police vehicle transporting a member of one of Portland's more notorious gangs, killing the gang member and a senior detective in charge of the City's gang unit, while also seriously injuring a homicide detective. The suspect in that case, Michael Moody, has been arrested and charged with a wide variety of crimes, including two counts of murder, one count of attempted murder, and various terrorism-related charges.

He has agreed to plead guilty and has agreed to testify against the Hoover Street Gang who, he alleges, hired him to kill one of their own. I want to talk more about that case, but we really need to discuss the other case we've been following.

As you will recall, we've been investigating the suspicious death of Portland socialite Charlene Price Davies. By way of background, Charlene was found dead at the bottom of the stairs at her mansion on N.E. Alameda Street, a home she shared with her second husband Dr. James Matthew Davies.

Last week, you heard my interview with Emad Aboujaoude, a circulating nurse who worked with Dr. Davies before he met and married Charlene. Emad told us how he suspected that Dr. Davies murdered a patient while he was undergoing a routine heart bypass operation. Unfortunately, by the time Emad disclosed his suspicions, too much time had passed, and the police didn't even bother with an investigation.

So, this is where the facts get really convoluted. The man who died during the operation was Ken Price, an early Nike executive and the husband of the recently deceased Charlene. Yes, that's right, Charlene married the anesthesiologist who is now suspected of killing her first husband.

Okay, are you still following? The main players in this Byzantine love triangle are Charlene, her first husband, Ken Price, and her second husband, Dr. James Davies. I should mention that we have no belief whatsoever that Charlene knew that Dr. Davies might have been responsible for her first husband's death. As far as we can tell, Ken and Charlene had a stable and loving marriage, although the same cannot be said about her marriage to Dr. Davies.

So now the question is how did Charlene and Dr. Davies come to marry one another? Well, the key figure for that is Portland's own lawyer to the wealthy and influential—Randy Wilkerson. Randy is a partner in the boutique law firm of Thrower, Kehoe, Wilkerson & Jada. He is widely considered one of the best estate planning attorneys in the Northwest and has represented pretty much everyone who is anyone in Oregon or otherwise has deep enough pockets to afford him. Randy has also been known in the gossip columns as being Portland's most eligible bachelor over the past couple of decades.

Randy and Dr. Davies go all the way back to college and, despite very different personalities and career paths, appear to have maintained a very close friendship over the past thirty plus years. We've learned that after an appropriate mourning period, Randy introduced Dr. Davies to Charlene and, in less than a year, they were married.

Now that you know all the players, I need to go off on a tangent that further entangles these people. As we discussed in Episode Two, Randy had drafted a trust agreement for Ken and Charlene Price. This trust, involving in excess of forty million dollars, was intended to benefit Charlene, should Ken pass first, and their daughter Kelly. Uncharacteristically for someone of Randy Wilkerson's legal acumen, however, the trust agreement contained a number of errors.

Most importantly, the trust agreement allowed Charlene to add a new beneficiary, even to the detriment of her daughter and that is exactly what she did. After marrying Dr. Davies and only shortly before she died, she added him as a beneficiary to this multi-million-dollar trust. While the daughter continued to receive a sizable monthly stipend, she did not inherit the balance of the trust when her mother passed. Instead, the trust continues for the benefit of Dr. Davies until he passes.

As I was unraveling all of this, I got this odd feeling that something wasn't right but couldn't place my finger on it. Might Randy Wilkerson have intentionally erred in drafting the trust agreement and then steered Charlene and Dr. Davies together in order to help his friend? Could Dr. Davies have killed Charlene's husband Ken as part of a conspiracy with Randy to obtain access to the millions in the trust? All these thoughts and suspicions came to me and, quite frankly, resulted in more than a few sleepless nights.

Oh, did I mention that in addition to drafting the defective trust agreement, Randy also serves as its trustee and gets paid handsomely for doing so?

Dear listeners, in all the years that I've been involved in podcasting, as well as my time in law enforcement, I've never seen anything quite so convoluted. Every thread that I pull seems to lead to a different thread in another part of the fabric.

With all of this information, I thought it reasonable to do a little more research on the Silver Fox himself, Randy Wilkerson. I reached out to, and spoke with, a number of his classmates back at the University of Washington and they were all very cooperative. Wilkerson was born in Tulsa, Oklahoma. He attended UW on a track scholarship and was very popular. These classmates remembered both Randy and Dr. Davies, and they always marveled at their friendship due to the differences in their respective personalities. Randy was always very flamboyant and extroverted, while Davies was very reserved and quiet.

They apparently became friends when they were both involved in UW's theater department. They were cast in various productions, usually with Randy as a lead character and Davies in more supporting roles.

After graduation, Randy attended the University of Oregon Law School and then he built his legal career in the Portland metropolitan area. He was known for dating a wide range of women, often models and wealthy widows. There were never any serious relationships, just a revolving door of attractive young and then middle-aged women.

I was told about his strong friendship with Charlene and how they used to attend various charitable events and galas together as Dr. Davies had no interest in doing so.

In the last year, however, someone finally hooked him, and he had fallen madly in love. It was a very hush-hush affair, involving discreet rendezvouses outside of the Portland metropolitan region. They would often go to Yamhill County's smaller and more-remote wineries, where they would be less likely to be recognized.

By all accounts Randy was smitten with this woman and it is believed that he was going to propose to her. He took his love to ōkta restaurant in McMinnville but, apparently, it didn't go as planned and she declined his proposal. She was married and wanted to give her marriage a second try.

So, who was this woman? The woman who had finally gotten Portland's most eligible bachelor to propose. I'll let you know as soon as we get back from this word from our sponsors.

Meg sat back and took a deep breath.

"That was great, Meg."

"Thanks. How about another quick shot before we continue? I see there's still tequila in the bottle."

Joyce McCarthy smiled, shook her head, and then leaned over and gave Meg a gentle kiss upon her cheek. "Later, Meg, later."

CHAPTER THIRTY-ONE

Karb knocked on the door.

"Come in."

The two detectives walked in as the captain watched them. He motioned for them to sit down.

"Sorry to bother you, Captain," Karb began, "but we've had a development in the Charlene Davies' case that we thought you should be aware of."

"Okay," the captain said and leaned back in his chair, clasping his hands on his stomach.

"Well, we've been investigating the husband…"

The captain interrupted, "Despite the fact that we still can't definitively establish that she was murdered, as opposed to just accidentally falling down the stairs."

The two men looked at one another. Karb knew he had once been friends with the captain but that was now apparently over. He knew that he'd made the captain's life more difficult over the past year, but the open hostility seemed excessive, even for that.

"Captain," Karb said, his voice noticeably quieter, "do we have a problem?"

The captain jerked up in his chair. "Of course we have a problem. You've been spending your time and this department's resources chasing a case that you can't prove, a case you can't even establish was a murder. So, in answer to your question, yes, Detective, we have a problem."

Capobianco spoke up, "With all due respect, sir, we believe that there *was* a murder. We have a couple of new developments that we think you should be aware of."

"Alright," the captain replied, slowly settling back into his chair again. "What are they?"

"Well, sir, we were checking the victim's phone records and she received a call right at 2:00 am on the morning she died."

"Who was the call from?"

"That's one of the odd things, sir. It was from Randy Wilkerson."

"The lawyer? Why would he be calling her at that time of night?"

This time, Karb responded. "That's the thing. He called her from the driveway of the Davies' house. We have Ring video of him pulling into the driveway at 1:55 am and sitting in the car for ten minutes."

Karb noted that the hostility in the captain's eyes had been replaced by a look of curiosity. "At 2:05 am, Wilkerson got out of his car and walked into the house. It appears that he used a key to get in."

"Were any lights turned on?" the captain asked.

Karb continued, "No, he was in there for seven minutes before he walked back out. He was moving at a quick pace, although not running, and drove away."

The captain looked at the two detectives and opened his mouth to say something when they all heard a telephone ring. Capobianco reached for her cellphone as the two men stared at her. She looked at the phone and then promptly hit the button to refuse it.

"Detective, really? I thought we had an understanding that telephones would be put on silent before you came into my office."

Capobianco said, "Absolutely, sir, I'm so sorry. I just forgot."

Her cellphone then rang again.

"Detective!" the captain said sharply as Capobianco again reached for her phone.

Capobianco looked at the phone and this time let it continue to ring.

"Sir, it's Debbie Pedersen. She wouldn't be calling me twice if it wasn't important."

The captain just stared at her as she hit the answer button and put the phone up to her ear.

"Yes, Debbie?"

"Capo, where are you?"

"Bill and I are meeting with the captain."

"Oh, good. Put me on speaker."

With a puzzled look, Capobianco pushed the speaker button on her phone and placed it on the captain's desk.

"Captain, I'm sorry to interrupt but I need to ask if any of you have listened to Meg Nguyen's podcast today."

The two detectives and the captain all said nothing but just stared at one another.

"Okay, I'll take that as a no. She says that the Davies woman was having an affair before she died. The affair was apparently with Randy Wilkerson."

The captain leaned forward towards the cellphone on his desk. "Say that again, Debbie."

"Meg says that Wilkerson and Charlene Davies were having a serious affair but that she broke it off just a couple of days before she died."

The captain continued, "Did she say how she knows this?"

"No sir, but I can reach out to her. She's usually pretty reliable with her info before she puts something like that out on the air. Have we considered that Wilkerson might have killed her rather than the husband?"

"Karb and Capo just told me that Wilkerson was at the house right about the time she died."

There was silence as he continued to look at the cellphone.

"Jesus! Okay, I'll reach out to Meg and see what she'll tell me."

"No, you won't," the captain quickly responded. "You're still on leave while you recover. Capo, you have a relationship with Nguyen, don't you?"

"I'm not sure it's much of a relationship right now but…"

"Yeah, I don't care. Contact Nguyen. See if she'll cooperate and tell you how she figured out Wilkerson and Charlene were romantically involved."

"Captain, she generally wants a trade of information if she's going to give up something. Can I tell her that we have evidence about Wilkerson being at the house about the time the wife was killed?"

"Absolutely not! We need to get Wilkerson in here for questioning before any of that gets out. We don't want to let him know what we know. With the information from Nguyen, we have enough to call him in. Let's see if he'll tell us anything about where he was that night. As for Nguyen, tell her you might have some information but can't share it with her just yet."

The captain picked up Capobianco's cellphone and said, "Okay, Debbie, thanks for the info." He paused for a minute and then his voice changed timbre slightly. "How's the recovery coming along?"

"Slowly. They've promised to get me a prosthetic, but I can't be fitted for it until the wound is fully healed. It will be another few weeks before that happens."

"Okay, have you started counseling yet?" the captain asked.

There was silence.

"Debbie, I asked if you've started counseling yet?"

"No, sir."

"Okay, Debbie, take as much time as you need but remember that I won't allow you to return until you've had a full physical and mental health evaluation and are cleared. You were blown up and lost a leg and an eye, damn it, that's enough to scramble anyone's psyche. Get it scheduled and soon. Wc want you back here."

"Thank you, sir, I will."

Capobianco's cellphone then went silent, and the captain picked it up and handed it back to Capobianco. The three of them looked at one another.

"Bill, reach out to Wilkerson and ask if he'll come down to the station voluntarily for questioning. Capo, let me know what Nguyen says."

The two detectives stood up and Karb asked, "Captain, this complicates things, doesn't it, at least as long as the husband is still a viable suspect?"

"Of course, it does! God damn it! I'll reach out to the ADA and get her involved again. In the meantime, see if you can figure out a way to rule out Dr. Davies as a suspect."

"Yes, sir."

The two detectives turned and walked back to their desks, Capobianco closing the captain's door behind them.

Chapter Thirty-Two

"Mr. Wilkerson, Mr. Thrower asked that you meet him in the large conference room as soon as you get back in."

"Jesus, LaVonne, can I at least take off my coat first?"

"I'm sorry sir, but he said it was important."

"Did he say what it was about?" Wilkerson asked with his back turned to his legal assistant and as he placed his jacket on the valet stand beside his credenza.

"No, sir. He just said it was important."

"Alright. When I get back, I'll need to see the Ronda Divers file, as well as the Baloun file."

"Yes, sir."

Wilkerson walked out the door and to the conference room which was just down the hallway from the reception area. It was large with a video screen on one end and a polished maple bookshelf on the other. The bookshelf was full of legal treatises that looked impressive but were rarely, if ever, used now that most legal research was done online.

He noticed that in addition to Rufus Thrower III, who was sitting at the head of the table, Matthew Kehoe was on one side and Bahij Jada was on the other. Thrower, who generally went by Trey, was a tall black man with braided hair which, along with his goatee, was starting to show a touch of gray. He wore horn-rimmed glasses and a dark gray suit with a green tie.

Before Wilkerson could say a word, Thrower said, "Randy, please sit down." Wilkerson recognized that this wasn't a request but a command. He had seen Thrower use this tone of voice to great effect with juries and other attorneys but had never experienced it directed at him. He sat down at the far end of the conference table.

"This looks serious," Wilkerson said with a tone of bemusement and a slight smile on his face. The other attorneys instantly recognized it as the start of Wilkerson's standard charm offensive.

"We have a question for you. Were you having an affair with Charlene Davies?"

The smile instantly disappeared from Wilkerson's mouth. "I'm not sure that's any of your business."

"Cut the crap, Randy." This was Matthew Kehoe. He was a slender man with a large bald head. He was known in equal parts for his intellect and his temper. "How the hell could you sleep with a client? You know you can't do that!"

Wilkerson shrugged his shoulders and merely said, "I guess the heart wants what the heart wants."

"Really?" asked Thrower. "With all of this going on, you sleep with a client, one whose estate plan you screwed up, and then you make some casual quip? By the way, when were you going to tell us that you screwed up the trust agreement?"

"First of all, that wasn't me. You know the kid screwed up the trust agreement…"

"And you should have caught it. You were his supervising attorney, and it was your responsibility to check his work, especially on a trust the size of Ken Price's. Okay, let me tell you how this proceeds…"

Just then, all three men turned as they heard loud arguing in the reception area. To their collective surprise, Dr. James Davies stormed into the conference room. He saw the three men and immediately headed directly for Wilkerson.

"You son of a bitch! I knew she was seeing someone, but I never thought it was you. You were supposed to be my best friend. How the fuck could you do that to me?"

Wilkerson stood up and put his arms out to fend off Davies. "Jim, listen to me, I…"

He couldn't finish as Davies' right fist swung up and connected solidly with Wilkerson's left cheek, knocking him back in his chair. Kehoe was up in a moment and grabbed Davies by the arms before he could get another swing in.

"I'm going to kill you! I don't care what it takes but I'm going to get you and make sure you burn in hell! You miserable, lying motherfucker!"

Kehoe, still holding on to Davies, slowly started to move him back towards the door and spoke softly to him. "Dr. Davies, he's not worth it. I promise, he'll get what's coming to him but he's not worth it. Take a breath."

Kehoe slowly loosened his grip as he felt Davies' body start to sag.

With tears starting to well up in his eyes, Davies continued addressing Wilkerson. "After everything we've been through, I can't believe you were the one. Randy, how could you do this to me?"

Wilkerson, holding his hands up to his face, said nothing but just bowed his head. Kehoe slowly turned Davies around and escorted him out of the conference room. The receptionist had the telephone in her hand and asked Kehoe, "Should I call the police?"

Kehoe looked at Davies and saw a man who was completely deflated. His anger was replaced by emotional exhaustion and tears were starting to run down his cheeks.

"No, Gwen, that won't be necessary." Turning back to Davies, Kehoe said in a very soft voice, "Doctor, you have my sincerest apologies for Randy's actions. We are dealing with it on our end, and you should consult with an attorney to find out what your options are. Whatever you do, stay away from Randy. People heard you threaten him, and should anything happen to him, you'll be the lead suspect. You don't need that.

"Go home, have a drink, and then find an attorney. I can't recommend one but, if you don't know one, you should ask your friends or contact the Oregon State Bar. They have a lawyer referral service."

Davies looked at Kehoe, pulled a handkerchief out of his back pocket and dabbed at his eyes and cheeks, before blowing his nose. He turned and walked out the front door of the law firm without saying anything else.

As Kehoe turned back towards the conference room, he said, "Gwen, get Mr. Wilkerson a bag of ice, please."

"Yes, sir."

As Kehoe walked back in the conference room, he saw that Wilkerson was still holding his hands to his face but was sitting up straight in his chair. Bahij Jada and Trey Thrower were just returning to their chairs as Kehoe walked to his.

Thrower began speaking. "Okay, Randy, this is how it is going to go. You are going to resign from the firm, and we will cash out your interest, consistent with our partnership agreement."

Wilkerson pulled his hands down from his cheek, a look of shock on his face. "You can't do this!"

Trey Thrower didn't let him get any further. "Randy, do you have any idea how this plays out?"

Wilkerson responded, "I brought in almost forty percent of the firm's billings last year. You can't kick me out."

Thrower calmly continued. "I assume that the Bar will initiate an investigation, either on its own or after Dr. Davies files a complaint. Rule 1.8(j) of the Oregon Rules of Professional Conduct expressly prohibits an attorney from having sexual relations with a client, especially in circumstances such as this. At a minimum, your license will be suspended.

"More importantly for the firm, no client in their right mind will ever trust this firm again with their estate planning. The media will jump on the news that a name partner in our firm was having an affair with a client, especially a married woman…a woman married to the attorney's supposed best friend.

"Most importantly, however, is that I expect you and the firm to be sued by Kelly Price. As soon as she learns of your malpractice in the drafting of her father's trust agreement, and we are obligated to notify her of that, our exposure will be in excess of $30,000,000. We, of course, have excess malpractice coverage but nowhere near enough to cover that."

Thrower paused just long enough for Wilkerson to look at Bahij Jada and say, "Bahij, help me here. We've been friends for a long time, hell, I was even in your wedding."

The look on Bahij's face was a combination of disgust and anger, although mostly anger. "Randy, you asked me to represent Dr. Davies when you had been having an affair with his wife. Do you have any idea how fucked up that is?"

Wilkerson averted his eyes.

Trey Thrower stood up. "Randy, you'll leave the office right now. We'll box up your personal effects and have them delivered to your home by the end of the day."

"But I need to get my jacket and my keys."

"Mrs. Floyd is right outside the door with both of those items. Goodbye Randy. You should talk to an attorney as soon as possible; you're going to need one."

Wilkerson stood up, looking like a completely defeated man and nothing like the titan who had stridden through the halls of Thrower, Kehoe, Wilkerson & Jada just moments before. As he exited the door, he saw his now former legal assistant holding his jacket in one hand and his keys in the other.

"You knew?" he asked her, but she didn't respond.

Grabbing his jacket and keys, he walked out the door, desperately trying to maintain whatever dignity he might have left.

CHAPTER THIRTY-THREE

"Bill, why are you so wound up?"

Karb looked at Dr. Malone and asked, "What do you mean?"

"Well, let's see—you're sitting on the edge of your chair, and I can see your right knee going up and down, up and down. Your hands seem to be moving nervously. It doesn't take a police detective to see that something is up with you. What is it?"

Karb took a deep breath, settled back in the chair across the desk from Dr. Malone and forced himself to be still.

"It's this case I'm working on. There are some new developments that I'm still trying to figure out. It's really convoluted."

"Want to talk about it?"

"I can't; this is part of a police investigation."

"Bill, to the extent that the case impacts your mental health, which is so obviously does, it is protected by the doctor-client privilege. So again, why are you so wound up?"

"You may have heard of the woman, Charlene Price Davies, who died a few months ago?"

"I have, but mostly because I've been listening to the *Murder in Bridge City* podcast."

She could see Karb bristle at the mention of the podcast. He wondered to himself if everyone, other than himself, listened to that damn thing.

"I heard that she was having an affair with everyone's favorite hot old guy, Randy Wilkerson."

Karb laughed. "I like you calling him an old guy. He's got a pretty big ego and still thinks he's in his thirties or forties."

"Bill, it doesn't matter if he's in his fifties or even older, he's still awfully damn good looking. So, he was having an affair with his best friend's wife. Other than it being tawdry, why are you so agitated?"

Karb paused. He didn't feel comfortable disclosing details of the investigation to anyone outside of the department, even if it was privileged.

"It looks like he was at the Davies' house at or about the time that Charlene died."

Dr. Malone sat up straight, a look of surprise on her face. "Could he have killed her?"

"It's certainly possible and that's what we are investigating. This part of a murder investigation is always the most interesting and difficult for me. It's like putting a puzzle together and the pieces are starting to come together quickly. Of course, it might be easier if Captain Schnadig wasn't riding my ass."

"What is he doing?"

Karb hesitated again. Finally, he continued, "We met with him yesterday and he was pissed off at me."

"Do you have any idea why?"

Karb shook his head from side to side. "I have no idea. I mean I understand that I've made his life more difficult over the last year or so—hence why I'm here—but I haven't done anything lately that should have pissed him off."

"What did he say?"

"He didn't say anything expressly. It's just that he was so openly hostile to me. Even Capo noticed."

Dr. Malone put down her notepad on the desk and leaned forward. "Bill, if you haven't done anything recently that would set him off, why do you assume that it was you who pissed him off?"

"What do you mean?"

"Look, Bill, you've been through a lot of traumas in your life, and I would never discount the effect those have had on you. You surely know, however, that you are not the only person who has suffered traumas."

She took a moment to look at him and she could see he was trying to process what she was saying.

"There is a saying that no one gets through this life unscathed. Captain Schnadig certainly has experienced his share of trauma but maybe it isn't even that. Maybe he had a fight with his husband that day or maybe someone close to him is ill, you just don't know. Maybe it is something as simple as him being chewed out by *his* boss and he was merely taking it out on you.

"We all do that sometimes. If we feel we can't yell at the person who has made us angry, we lash out at whomever is in our line of fire. So, could it be something as simple as the captain just having a bad day?"

Karb paused before responding. "I guess."

"Well, Bill, if you don't think you did anything that would have made him angry, isn't it more likely that something else did and you're just the convenient whipping boy?"

Karb took a deep breath and turned his head to look at the artwork on the wall. It gave him enough time to let her words sink in and he realized she was probably right. Unbeknownst to him, a small smile appeared on his lips.

Turning back, he said, "Doc, I get it. Do you mind if we cut today's session a bit short? I've got a meeting with the captain and the ADA later today and I'd like some more time to prep."

"I think we can do that but first, have you done anything social of late?"

Karb smiled and said, "I took Coach out for dinner the other day. He's been so supportive that I figured it's the least I could do."

"Where did you go?"

"He's Italian so I took him to this little place over on N.E. 28th called Montelupo."

"I've never heard of it. Did he like it?"

"Well, he said he did so I'm going to take him at his word."

"Good for you, Bill. How about joining a book club or maybe a hiking group?"

Karb shook his head in a noncommittal way. "Actually, I was thinking about buying a Harley and maybe finding a group to ride with."

"I think that's a great idea. Let me know what you decide next time we meet."

Karb stood up and as he turned toward the door, he waved his hand and said, "Thanks, Doc."

Dr. Malone watched him leave and then picked up her Dictaphone.

❧

Chapter Thirty-Four

The four of them, Karb, Capobianco, Captain Schnadig, and Assistant District Attorney Laura Iwasaki, sat around the table looking at the white board on the wall in front of them. At the top of the board was scrawled one name—*Charlene Price Davies*. Just a few inches below that and on either side of her name were two columns with the names *Randy Wilkerson* and *James Davies* at the top of each.

Just below their names and in the middle of the board was the word *MOTIVE*.

Underneath Wilkerson's name was written *Spurned Lover*. Under Davies' name was written *Money*.

The next row down had MEANS written in the middle of the board. Large check marks were resting beneath the names of both of the suspects.

The next row down had OPPORTUNITY written in the middle of the board. Again, large check marks rested in each column.

"God damn it!" ADA Iwasaki growled, slamming her hand down on the table. "Okay, let's go through each one again."

Karb rubbed his eyes in both frustration and fatigue but stood up.

"Dr. James Matthew Davies; husband of the victim. His motive could be money. He and Charlene were the beneficiaries of a large multi-million-dollar trust, but Charlene had the ability to cut him out if she wanted to. She'd had an affair, and their marriage was less than ideal. By killing her, the trust becomes irrevocable, and he is the primary beneficiary. He becomes financially secure."

"Means!" Iwasaki blurted out.

"There is evidence that he taped some sort of string at the top of the stairs to trip her in the middle of the night."

"Nope," Iwasaki said angrily. "The uniform's testimony will be weak in that he didn't secure the scene and didn't seize the tape and string. Davies' attorney will crush him on cross- examination. Hell, a first-year law student would crush him on cross-examination."

"The petechiae clusters around the mouth, nose, and eyes suggest that she may have been suffocated after she fell; bruising on her arms is suggestive of DV."

"Not conclusive," Iwasaki again interjected. "The petechiae clusters could have been the result of her suffocating from the fall, not from someone smothering her. The DV is speculative, and no judge will allow that in without testimony of a witness…but we don't have any witnesses to abuse, do we?"

Karb shook his head no.

"Opportunity!" Iwasaki belted out, far too loud than was necessary.

"He was home," Karb responded. "He says he didn't hear her fall, but he certainly could have walked down the stairs after tripping her and finished the job."

"Objection!" Iwasaki spit out. "Speculative."

"Okay," she continued after taking a sip of water to regain her composure. "Go through Wilkerson."

Karb pointed to the board. "He had motive. We can establish that he had a lengthy and heated affair with the victim. She broke it off only a few days before her death."

He looked at Iwasaki and she nodded.

"As to means and opportunity, he was at the house at or about the time of her death. We can affirmatively place him at the scene of the crime."

Iwasaki rubbed her face and said, "But he wasn't alone at the house, was he?"

"No, ma'am." Karb looked at her to see if she had anything else to say. When she didn't, he looked at Captain Schnadig who just stared at him with no emotion. Karb then looked at Capobianco and she shrugged her shoulders.

Iwasaki stood up and walked to the white board. After staring at it for almost a minute and without turning around, she said, "Okay, folks. We have two potential suspects, and that fact creates a reasonable doubt for each of them."

She then turned around and placed her hands on her hips. "I want you to dig and figure out how I can absolutely and positively rule one of these guys out. I can't charge them both and I can't charge either one at this point because I won't be able to prove, beyond a reasonable doubt, that one killed her and the other didn't. I don't know how you do it but you better figure this out or one of these guys is going to get away with murder."

Chapter Thirty-Five

"Bill, any suggestions?"

"I'll go and talk to Wilkerson. Maybe he'll agree to come down here for a full interview. I doubt it, but we have to try. Why don't you contact Davies' attorney and see if he and Davies will come in. We can try telling each of them that the other is talking, and maybe one will crack and give us something."

"Bill, if you really believe that, you've got a lot more optimism than I do."

Karb gave a snort and said, "Nah, I don't expect either of them to give up the other, but we have to try something. Given how he attacked Wilkerson the other day, there's at least a chance that Davies might be able to give us something to hang Wilkerson with."

Karb stood up and started walking towards the elevator. Capobianco called out "good luck" as he got in. Karb headed up to PacWest Center and the offices of Thrower, Kehoe, Wilkerson & Jada, P.C.

It was only a few blocks and he rehearsed what he wanted to say to Wilkerson when he got there. The elevator was crammed with lawyers and accountants returning from lunch. Karb noted that at least one of his companions in the elevator had consumed far too much garlic recently.

The elevator door opened, and he allowed two middle-aged women to exit first. He turned to his left and noticed a man working on the law firm's signage on the glass door. He softly coughed and the workman looked up and moved aside to allow Karb to enter.

He immediately noticed that the signage above the receptionist desk now just read "Thrower, Kehoe & Jada, P.C." Quickly walking up to the receptionist, he waited for her to finish the call she was on and hang the phone up.

"May I help you, sir?"

"Yes, I'm Detective Bill Karb with the Portland Police Department. I was wondering if I could see Randy Wilkerson."

The receptionist's face turned red, and she stammered, "I'm sorry, sir, but Mr. Wilkerson no longer works here. Let me call for Mr. Thrower. I'm sure he can talk to you."

Karb looked at the young woman. "Sure, that'll be fine."

As the receptionist picked up the phone, Karb took a look around the office. They certainly hadn't wasted any time in removing Wilkerson from the firm. He could understand why. The old adage about even bad publicity being good publicity apparently didn't apply to law firms. He sat down in one of the leather chairs and pulled out his phone. He quickly texted Capobianco saying, "Wilkerson's been canned by the law firm."

Just then, a tall black man walked into the reception area and stood before him. "Good afternoon, I am Rufus Throwers III, the managing partner here. I understand you asked about Randy Wilkerson?"

Karb stood up, put out his hand and shook Thrower's. "I'm Detective Bill Karb, Portland PD. Can we talk for a minute?"

Thrower nodded and turned towards the receptionist. "Gwen, we'll be in the small conference room."

She nodded her head and started typing something on her computer.

The two men walked into the conference room and sat down at an oval-shaped maple table facing one another.

Karb began, "It looks like you didn't waste any time cutting ties with Wilkerson."

"Detective Karb, the partners made a decision, and it was mutually agreed that Mr. Wilkerson should continue his career elsewhere."

"Care to tell me why that decision was made now?"

Thrower looked at him and just said, "No, I don't. That would seem to be a question better posed to Mr. Wilkerson."

"Fair enough, any idea where I might find him?"

With no change in intonation, Thrower merely responded "I'm sure I have no idea."

The two men just sat and stared at each other. While Karb hoped he might be able to stare this man down, he knew that you didn't become a senior partner at a successful law firm by being intimidated.

"May I talk to Wilkerson's assistant?"

"I'm sorry, Detective, but she is busy. As you might imagine, we have a lot of work going on with Mr. Wilkerson's sudden departure. Perhaps you can contact her after hours."

"Can you give me her name and phone number then?" Karb asked.

"I'm sorry, Detective, but I don't feel comfortable giving out that information without her consent."

Karb knew that he wasn't going to get any cooperation, so he stood up. Reaching into his pocket, he pulled out a business card and handed it to Thrower.

"Well, if you think of anything you'd like to tell me about Wilkerson or if the assistant is willing to speak with me, here's my card."

Standing up, Thrower responded, "Of course, Detective."

He then stood and walked out the conference room door, holding the door open for Karb to exit. Karb did just that, got into the elevator, and quickly descended to the building's lobby. Stepping out of the elevator, Karb called Capobianco.

"Capo, any luck with Davies?"

"No," she responded. "Apparently he's no longer represented by Bahij Jada and Jada couldn't, or *wouldn't,* tell me who Davies' new attorney is."

"Yeah, that figures. Wilkerson's out of the firm and they must be cutting all ties with him and Davies."

"Did you get any info on why Wilkerson is out?"

"No, but it was quick. They're taking his name off the door right now. Hey, I know Wilkerson lives somewhere in the Pearl. Do you remember his address?"

"I don't but I can get it. I'll text it to you."

"Great, I'll go over there and see if I can talk to him. I'll meet you back at the station afterwards."

There was a pause before Capobianco said, "Bill, be careful. If he did kill Charlene and he just got canned from his firm, he might be more dangerous than we thought."

Even though she couldn't see it, Karb nodded his head in agreement and said, "Good point. Thanks."

He hung up and walked to his car. By the time he got there, Capobianco had texted him Wilkerson's address on Northwest 9th Avenue. Northeast Portland, between the Willamette River to the north, West Burnside to the south and between NW Broadway and the Interstate 405 Highway is commonly referred to as The Pearl District. In its past life, it had been occupied by warehouses, light industry, and rail yards but had recently been transformed through urban renewal to become one of the city's more popular mixed-use neighborhoods.

Parking his car on the street, Karb looked at the building in front of him. It was a thirteen-story building with a façade of silver metal and a lot of windows. Karb opened the tall glass door and walked into the lobby. It was large and cool, but with an odd antiseptic feeling to it. Walking over to the directory, he noted a security guard sitting there.

Pulling out his badge, Karb said, "Detective Bill Karb, Portland PD. I'm here to see Randy Wilkerson."

The guard did not appear to be unsettled by the appearance of a police detective.

"Is Mr. Wilkerson expecting you?"

Karb smiled.

"No, no he isn't."

"Very well, Detective. I'll have to call Mr. Wilkerson to see if I should send you up."

Karb nodded and the guard picked up his phone. "Mr. Wilkerson, there's a police detective here who would like to speak with you."

The guard paused as he listened to the other voice on the phone. "Yes, sir." Looking up at the detective, he said, "Mr. Wilkerson said he'll be down shortly. You can wait over there." He pointed to a sterile leather and chrome couch across the lobby.

With a nod of his head, Karb walked over to the couch and sat down. He knew how this scenario played out. Wilkerson would take his time coming down in hopes that Karb would get tired of waiting and leave. If that was, in fact, Wilkerson's plan, it would fail because Karb could be very patient when he wanted to be.

It was fifty-five minutes before Karb heard the ding of the elevator and watched as Randy Wilkerson strode across the lobby. Holding out his hand as he approached, Wilkerson said, "Detective, I'm so sorry to keep you waiting. It's been quite the day."

Karb stood and shook Wilkerson's hand. He handed him his business card and asked, "Mr. Wilkerson, I'm working on an investigation of the death of Charlene Price and was wondering if you'd be willing to come down to the station and let me formally interview you."

"Oh, Detective, am I a suspect?"

Karb fought to not bristle at the condescending tone of Wilkerson's question.

"With all due respect, Mr. Wilkerson, it might be better if we discuss this down at the station."

"The question is—am I a suspect? The answer to that should be as simple as saying yes or no. Your answer to *my* question will likely determine my response to *your* question." The tone of Wilkerson's voice had become more aggressive.

"Sir, I would say that you are a person of interest, and we hope we can get that out of the way if you'll come in and talk with me."

Wilkerson looked at the detective in front of him. He clearly noticed the scuffed shoes and the suit that couldn't be less than ten years old and, even then, couldn't have cost more than $250.00.

"I'm sorry, Detective, but I've got a lot to do and just don't have the time right now." He then leaned in and with an almost conspiratorial voice added, "And, further, I really don't have the inclination to help you."

Standing back up straight, Wilkerson looked at the detective who just stared back at him.

"Have a good day, Detective," Wilkerson said and then turned and walked back to the elevator.

As Karb was walking back to his car, he muttered to himself, "Fat lot of good that did."

❧

Back at the station, Capobianco retreated into one of the vacant interrogation rooms. She sat down and picked up her cellphone. She dialed the number and waited for the call to be answered.

"Hey, Capo, to what do I owe this honor?"

"Meg, I need to know how you found out that Wilkerson was sleeping with Charlene Price Davies."

"I can't tell you that, but I can give you some info regarding their breakup."

Capobianco, sounding annoyed, replied, "Yeah, I heard about that. It was out at that fancy restaurant in McMinnville."

"But what I didn't mention on the podcast is that Wilkerson apparently got physical when she broke things off. One of the waiters told me that he grabbed Charlene's arm and hauled her out of her seat. He was yelling before the maître d' came over and asked him to leave. They then called an Uber for Charlene."

"Why didn't you mention that in the podcast?"

"Joyce and I made the decision that we already had enough going on and didn't want to get bogged down in too many details."

"Is there anything else you can tell me?"

"I'm sorry, Capo, but there's just nothing else right now. Like you, we're running down leads."

"Okay, thanks." Capobianco hung up and walked back to the conference room where they had met earlier in the day with the captain and the ADA. Going over to the white board, it still contained the two columns headed by "Davies" and "Wilkerson." Under the "Means" heading in Wilkerson's column, Capobianco wrote "Violence at Okta; bruises on vic's arm."

She then stood back and studied the board. As hard as she tried, she still couldn't figure out what had really happened to Charlene Price Davies.

CHAPTER THIRTY-SIX

Welcome to Season Four of Murder in Bridge City, *my podcast for those interested in exploring the violent and ugly underbelly of our fair city of Portland, Oregon. I am your host, Meg Nguyen, and this is Episode Four. I hope all of you are well and avoiding the dark side of our city of roses.*

Sometimes I like my job and other times I really, really like my job! This season, we've been following a couple of criminal investigations but the only one I'm going to talk about today is the murder of Charlene Price Davies.

Yes, I said murder. In previous episodes, I referred to her death as suspicious, but I am now convinced that she was murdered. The only question is who killed her. Initially, I thought it was her husband, Portland anesthesiologist Dr. James Davies. He has been implicated in the mysterious death of Ken Price, a longtime Nike executive who died during a routine heart operation in which Dr. Davies had been the anesthesiologist.

He certainly had enough motive to kill his wife. He was the named beneficiary on a recently purchased three-million-dollar life insurance policy of Charlene. He also stood to be the principal beneficiary of a multi-million-dollar trust if his wife died, much to the chagrin of

Kelly Price, the daughter of Ken and Charlene and the stepdaughter of Dr. Davies. While I generally try and be impartial about suspects, I have to tell you that Dr. Davies gives off some really creepy vibes. I haven't met him in person but everything I've learned about him, and everyone I've talked to about him, suggests that he has that certain something that makes the killing of his wife a very realistic possibility.

A second suspect has, however, reared his perfectly coifed head just recently. As we discussed in the last segment, Portland's tax and estate planning attorney to the rich and wealthy, Randy Wilkerson, was apparently having a torrid affair with the victim. In fact, it appears that Portland's longtime most eligible bachelor had finally fallen in love, only to have her break it off, and break his heart, only days before her murder.

Was there a lovers' spat? Could he not bear the rejection and decide to kill the one woman whom he'd ever really loved? So many questions and we'll dive into those shortly. Before doing so, I want to let you know about the recent happenings to Wilkerson. Apparently, his partners decided to part ways with him and booted him from the firm.

I have it on good authority that the Oregon State Bar has started an investigation into him with allegations of a number of serious violations of the Bar's Code of Ethics.

Before we start our deep dive into these latest developments and who might, or might not, have killed Charlene Price Davies, let's hear a quick word from our sponsors…

"Meg, you need to tamp down on the glee. I know you are excited about this case, but you don't want to come across as happy about it."

"Yeah, okay, Joyce. I'll take it down a notch."

Meg felt the buzzing of her phone in her pocket and took it out. "Hello?"

"Meg? This is Tuna. Can we talk?"

"I'm in the middle of recording the podcast. Can it wait?"

"Sure, give me a call when you're done."

The phone went dead before Meg could respond.

"What might he want?" asked Joyce.

"I have no idea, but I look forward to finding out. Tuna's not one to call me just to catch up. He likely either wants something or might have some information to share."

Meg then took a sip of water and settled back in her chair, adjusting the microphone slightly. She nodded at Joyce to start recording again.

Chapter Thirty-Seven

"So, any suggestions?"

"Yeah…no, not really." Karb's frustration was obvious in his voice. "Okay, let's try this. You focus on Wilkerson, and I'll focus on Davies. We'll review each other's notes and if either of us finds anything new, we let the other know. What do you think?"

"Well, it's better than nothing but why give me Wilkerson?"

Karb looked at her and smiled. "You mean other than the fact you think he's so good looking?"

Capobianco smiled back. "Yeah, other than that."

"Well, I've been focusing on him for the last week or so and maybe a fresh set of eyes might help. Same thing with you focusing mostly on Davies. Maybe one, or even both of us, missed something."

"That sounds like it's worth a shot."

Karb reached down to the papers on his desk and handed his notes over to his partner. Capobianco did the same thing and the two of them got to work. For the next forty-five minutes, they worked in silence. Capobianco broke it by saying, "Bill, did you know that Wilkerson sold his condo back in March?"

Karb looked up and wheeled his chair over to be able to look at Capobianco's computer screen. "No, I didn't. Check to see if he's purchased any other property recently."

Capobianco started typing and within less than a minute, said, "There's no record of him owning any real property in Oregon. What the hell does that mean? Didn't you see him at his condo the other day?"

Karb shook his head and responded, "Yeah, he must have been renting back the condo after the sale. We need to find out how long his leaseback is for. Who did he sell the condo to?"

Capobianco started typing with Karb looking over her shoulder. Finally, she said, "It's a company called Daraee Holdings, LLC. Its principal is a guy named Hafez Daraee; he lives in Lake Oswego. I'll make a phone call."

Wheeling his chair back to his desk, Karb started working on his computer, only briefly looking up to see Capobianco on her phone. He couldn't make out much from listening to just her side of the conversation. Once she hung up, she turned to Karb, and he to her.

"He says he bought it as an investment property and leased it back to Wilkerson on a six-month lease. He says he never met Wilkerson in person and never even heard of him other than as a tenant. So why does Wilkerson sell his condo just weeks before his lover unexpectedly dumps him? Do you think he was planning on running away with her if she said yes?"

Karb responded, "But why run away? They both have deep roots in Portland. Maybe he was planning on buying a new place with Charlene, thinking his condo might be too much of a bachelor pad for her?"

"Yeah, maybe. Damn, I'd like to ask him about this?"

"Me too, but he made it abundantly clear that he wasn't going to talk to us at all."

"Okay, let's bear this in mind and keep looking."

Karb turned back to his computer when his cellphone rang. He answered it with "Karb here."

"Detective Karb, this is Rufus Thrower III, we met the other day."

Karb turned toward Capobianco and snapped his fingers to get her attention. As she turned, he responded, "Of course, you're the managing partner at Thrower, Kehoe, Wilkerson & Jada."

"Well, it's just Thrower, Kehoe & Jada now but, yes, that's me."

"Okay, Mr. Thrower, what can I do for you?"

"Well, I received a phone call from the manager at the branch of Bank of America that we use."

"And?"

"Well, he wanted to talk about a trust account that Randy Wilkerson had set up for the Price Family Trust."

"That's the trust that he set up for Ken Price before he died?"

"That's the one. Well, Randy was managing the trust outside of the firm."

Karb was staring at Capobianco. "Mr. Thrower, do you mind if I put you on speaker so my partner can hear what we're talking about?"

There was silence and Karb and Capobianco stared at each other. Finally, he said, "That'll be alright."

Karb then placed his cellphone on his desk and hit the speaker button. "Okay, Mr. Thrower, you were telling me that you received a call from Bank of America about the Price Trust that Randy Wilkerson was managing outside of the firm."

"That's correct."

"Can you explain to us what it means that he was managing the trust outside of the firm?"

"Well, generally an attorney who drafted a trust agreement doesn't act as the trustee. It creates problems. If issues arise from the management of the trust, it can be difficult to differentiate between whether the attorney was providing legal services or trustee services."

Capobianco spoke up, "Mr. Thrower, this is Detective Capobianco. Why is it important to be able to differentiate?"

Thrower continued, "All Oregon attorneys are required to maintain malpractice insurance and that insurance only applies to legal malpractice. If a trustee breaches his fiduciary obligations to the beneficiaries of a trust, that is not covered by the malpractice insurance."

Karb took back over the conversation. "Okay, so Wilkerson was acting as both the attorney for the trust and also as the trustee. I assume you were aware of him acting in those dual roles."

"As a matter of fact, I wasn't until fairly recently. We would never have permitted that to happen if we knew of it. The risk to the firm is just too great for us to allow that."

"And so you found out from the phone call you received from the Bank of America?"

"Exactly."

Karb and Capobianco sat and waited for the attorney to continue.

"Well, the manager from the bank apparently didn't know that Randy was running the trust outside of the firm or that he was no longer with the firm. In any event, he called me to confirm a large transfer out of the investment department."

Capobianco was listening but also watching Karb and she could see him tensing up.

"How large of a transfer?" Karb asked.

After a slight pause, the voice over the cellphone said, "Thirty-seven million, six hundred, eighty-two thousand, six hundred dollars, and fifty-seven cents."

The exhale by both Karb and Capobianco was audible, and she quietly whispered, "Jesus Christ."

"Yes, that was my reaction as well," Thrower responded.

"Mr. Thrower, were you able to determine where the transfer went to?"

"The funds were sent to an account with Butterfield Bank in the Cayman Islands."

The two detectives stared at each other, neither of them really knowing what to say next.

"And because I know you want to know; we can't reverse the transaction, nor can we find out anything further about the bank account that received the funds."

With a deep breath, Karb finally said, "Thank you, Mr. Thrower. We may have some additional questions for you."

"Certainly, you know where to find me."

"Thank you, sir," said Capobianco as the cellphone went dead.

She spoke first. "Well, I guess we have our guy."

"Looks that way. Let's go down to the captain and get a warrant out."

Just then as he was standing up, Karb's cellphone started ringing again. "Damn it!"

Picking up his phone, he said, "Karb."

"Bill, this is Meg. Don't hang up."

"Meg, we're busy. I can't talk right now."

"Bill! Bill! Wilkerson is gone."

Taking a deep breath, Karb said, "Go on."

"He's traveling under a fake passport."

"Meg, how solid is this information?"

"Rock solid."

"What is the name he's traveling under?"

"I don't have that information."

"You don't have it, or you won't disclose it?"

"Does it matter?"

Karb held the phone to his ear for a moment as he formulated his thoughts. He then said, "Thanks" and hung up.

Chapter Thirty-Eight

"Okay, I'll let Iwasaki know and we'll get a warrant out for Wilkerson. It may be too late but that's all we can do. Capo, you and Bill go and pick up Davies. With Wilkerson gone and having stolen the money, he may be ripe to talk and tell us what really happened with his wife. He'll either confess or tell us that Wilkerson did it. In either case, we need to move quickly. Got it?"

The two detectives stood up, nodded, and strode out the door without responding further. They didn't bother speaking as they took the elevator to the parking garage, nor as they drove to the house on Alameda Street.

The house was dark as they pulled into the driveway. Walking quickly up to the front door, Capobianco rang the doorbell, while Karb knocked harshly. Waiting just a moment, Karb instinctively turned the doorknob. It turned and Karb slowly opened the door.

Without entering, Karb pushed the door wide open and yelled, "Dr. Davies? It's Detectives Karb and Capobianco of the Portland Police."

There was no response. The house was silent.

Karb took a step onto the Persian rug in the entry way and looked around. He saw the staircase on his right where Charlene Davies spent her last few moments of life. He looked to his left and saw the living room. While the drapes were mostly drawn, there was enough sunlight coming in to show a piece of paper and some other items on the coffee table in front of an embroidered sofa.

"Dr. Davies?" Karb called again as he took another step. "Bill?"

"Capo, this is a welfare check now. The unlocked door gives us a reasonable basis to be concerned."

Karb then walked into the living room and stared down at the coffee table. There was the piece of paper he'd seen from the doorway propped up against a white porcelain bowl filled with potpourri. Next to the bowl was a watch, a cell phone, and a wallet.

Karb reached into his pocket, took out a pair of nitrile gloves from his jacket pocket, and put them on. He picked up the piece of paper and read it out loud.

What's the point now? For whomever is reading this, I want to say a few things.

I did not kill my wife. Charlene was the only woman I have ever loved, and I don't care if you believe that or not.

I did not kill Ken Price. I always took great pride in my medical skills and while I may not have been perfect, I never intentionally hurt anyone.

Randy Wilkerson was my best friend and I trusted him. I never thought he was capable of such evil. He played me and apparently has been playing me and everyone else for years. He is a monster.

He killed my wife but somehow convinced me to protect him even though he never explained why he did it. I'm not sure why I chose to protect him, but wish I never had.

So, what's the point now? My wife is dead. The person I thought was my best friend turned out to be a liar and a murderer. My career is over as no one will ever hire me again.

If I can ask one favor, please let Kelly know that I really am sorry about her mom's death and for being such a bad stepfather. I just didn't know how to be any better.

I guess there is no point after all.

JMD

CHAPTER THIRTY-NINE

Meg took a large bite of her barbacoa taco. She was feeling pleased with herself, although Joyce had strongly recommended that she not come across as too cocky. She had, once again, beaten the cops to critical information but she needed to stay on their good side.

Across the table from her at Taqueria Portland on SE 8th Avenue in Portland were detectives Carol Capobianco and Bill Karb. Karb already had a look of impatience on his face and Capobianco had already spilled some of the sauce from her spicy pork sandwich on her lap.

"Meg, how did you get that info about the fake passport?"

"Capo, again, I can't reveal my sources." She let that sink in for a moment before continuing, "But this time, my source has allowed me to do so. Remember Mike Moody, the bomber who injured Debbie and killed the cop and the gangbanger?"

Karb responded first, "Of course, so what?"

"Well, he had been affiliated with the Patriot Boys but was doing the bombing job on his own. Ed Barron…"

Karb interjected, "Tuna."

Meg continued, "Yes, Tuna…well he was concerned that I might push Moody's affiliation with the Boys when talking about the bombing. He explained to me right after the incident that the Patriot Boys had nothing to do with the bombing; that Moody had done this totally off the books. He asked me to keep the Boys out of my reporting and given the info he gave me, and the fact that I never heard any suggestion that the Boys were involved, I agreed."

Capobianco, still trying to sop up the juice on her lap, said, "And by doing so, he owed you a favor."

"Exactly. My sources aren't just limited to the police. I talk to a lot of different people, many of whom are very unlikeable."

A voice behind them rang out, "What? You didn't wait for me?"

Meg, Karb and Capobianco all looked up and then smiles broke across their faces.

"Debbie!" Capobianco exclaimed.

Meg stood up and watched as Debra Pedersen rolled towards them in her wheelchair. "I didn't know you were coming today."

"I know," Pedersen responded, "I was dying of cabin fever and convinced Chuck to let me out and drive me here."

"Where is Chuck?" Capobianco asked.

"He's parking the car. I had to convince him that once he got me into this chair, I could handle going the rest of the way on my own."

"He's just being protective," Karb said.

"Oh, I know, but he's still driving me crazy. I'm not used to being so dependent upon someone and I don't like it."

Meg cleared her throat and the other three looked up.

"Debbie, is your wheelchair bedazzled?"

Pedersen laughed and said, "Yeah, my granddaughter thought it might make me look cool. What do you think?"

"Absolutely, very, very cool," Meg responded as Karb and Capobianco nodded.

"Have you thought about bedazzling the eyepatch?" Karb added.

All three women turned and stared at Karb.

Capobianco spoke first. "Who are you? Bill Karb doesn't use humor."

"Sorry," Karb responded as he looked down with a slight smile on his face.

"Okay, enough with the small talk, what did I miss?"

"Well, Meg here just explained to us how she did Tuna a solid by keeping the Patriot Boys out of her reporting about Moody and your bombing."

"That's interesting. Meg, I hope you got some good juice for doing that?"

"Oh, I absolutely did. Tuna called me a couple of weeks ago and told me that one of his friends had been approached regarding getting a fake ID. This wasn't particularly unusual, although the guy wanted the full meal deal identity packages—a new birth certificate, driver's license, and passport. With the Real ID licenses that Oregon uses and the various protections in passports after 9/11, he explained that it is difficult."

"But not impossible," Karb interjected.

"No, Bill, it's not impossible, but it is expensive."

"And this guy was Randy Wilkerson?" This was a rhetorical question by Karb as they all knew the answer.

"Exactly. It turns out that Wilkerson flew down to L.A. A source in TSA said a 'Christopher Lynch' then flew from LA to Mexico City. That is apparently Wilkerson's new alias. The passport photo matches Wilkerson. He hasn't been seen since."

"And Davies is dead?" Pedersen asked.

"Presumably," said Karb. "Davies' car was found just north of Maupin. It was parked at the bottom of the rafting run and just before you get to Sherar's Falls. A jacket and shoes, presumed to be his, was found just past the Falls, but no body has been recovered yet.

"The guys out in Deschutes County told me that a body going over the Falls might be found anywhere downstream on the river or even all the way up in the Columbia River. Many bodies are apparently never found; they get caught in the rocks or under tree limbs. If he did jump in the river, the assumption is that he would have drowned because no one makes it over Sherar's Falls. Apparently, you're not allowed to even raft over it. We don't have any witnesses though, just his card and the suicide note so we can't be sure."

"Did he have any affiliation with the Deschutes River or the Falls? Did he fish or raft on the Deschutes?" Debbie asked.

"To the best of our knowledge, the answer is no, although we did find some flyfishing gear in his garage so there's a possibility he was familiar with the area."

They all started eating their lunches as they each continued processing this information and what it would do to the investigation. Each seemed to be waiting for one of the others to talk first.

Capobianco broke the silence. "So we still don't know for sure who killed Charlene. Presumably it was Wilkerson, especially given what Davies said in the suicide note, but we still likely wouldn't be able to get a conviction because of the whole reasonable doubt thing. Of course, it could also be Davies but, again, we just don't know.

"At least with Wilkerson, we've got an international warrant out for grand theft, so when he resurfaces, we should be able to get him for that. Assuming he resurfaces in a country with an extradition treaty."

"Exactly," agreed Meg.

Capobianco nodded her head and took another bite of her taco, failing to notice or care that she spilled a more taco sauce on her shirt.

"So, what's next for you, Meg? Bill and I will get on to new cases, but what about you?"

"First of all, we'll wrap up this season of the podcast. This isn't the way I wanted it to end, but I can only do so much. After that, I promised Joyce a vacation before we start working on next season."

"Where are you going?" Karb asked.

"I'm thinking about Mexico, Joyce wants to spend some time on the beach."

"Yeah, but let me guess," Pedersen spoke up. "It'll be in Mexico City rather than Acapulco."

Meg smiled and shrugged her shoulders.

"May I ask that if you find out anything about what happened to Wilkerson, that'll you'll let us know?" Karb inquired.

"Bill, you know I am always willing to trade information with the police."

Karb had to smile at that comment and merely responded with, "Of course, of course."

"Debbie," Meg asked, "what are you going to tell people when they ask about your leg?"

Pedersen smiled and responded, "Well, for those who know me, I'll tell them the truth. For those that don't, I'll make up some story."

"A story?" Capobianco inquired. "Do tell."

"I've been working on a few different ones. My personal favorite is that I lost the leg in a poker game. I'll tell them that I had aces over queens, but the son-of-a-bitch pulled out four sixes. What do you think?"

"Debra Jane Pedersen! I am impressed," Meg said. "I had no idea you were so creative."

"Well, I've had time to think and, to tell you the truth, the pain meds may have aided my creativity just a bit."

Karb then spoke up, "Well, if you get a wooden peg for a prosthetic, between that and the eye patch, you can pull off a whole pirate detective thing."

Again, the three women turned and stared at Karb.

"Yeah, this whole humor thing isn't me. Sorry, I'll go back to my usual self."

Pedersen responded, "Oh God, Bill, don't do that!"

All three women laughed as Karb fidgeted uncomfortably.

With a smile on their faces, other than Karb, and with lunch completed, they said their goodbyes. Pedersen waved for her husband, who was sitting at a separate table, to help her back to the car. Meg waved as she walked out the door and Karb and Capobianco drove back to the station.

"Bill, do you think we'll ever hear from Wilkerson again?"

"Oh, I think so. You can only hide for so long. Even if we do, however, his prosecution will be handled by the Feds for the wire transfer and grand theft. I'm confident that he'll get his due someday."

"But will we ever find out which one killed Charlene?"

"I doubt it, Capo, and that really pisses me off."

Chapter Forty

"All rise, the Honorable John Shelton presiding."

Judge Shelton strode through the door and sat down, adjusting his robe as he did so. He looked out over the edge of his bench and stared at the litigants gathered before him.

He said, "Now is the time set for the sentencing in the matter entitled *United States of America v. Michael Moody*, Case Number 23-28865. Counsel, please identify yourselves."

"Good afternoon, your Honor, Leslie Westfall, Assistant U.S. attorney representing the United States."

Shelton turned to the other attorney and slightly tilted his head.

"Good afternoon, your Honor, my name is Annie Hegedus, and this is my client, Michael Moody."

"Thank you both, you may be seated. In reviewing the record, Mr. Moody pleaded guilty to two counts of murder and one count of attempted murder, as well as one count of manufacturing an explosive device, and a final count of engaging in domestic terrorism. The remaining fifteen charges were dismissed. Counsel, is that correct?"

Leslie Westfall stood up and politely said, "Yes, your Honor."

Ann Hegedus remained seated and just nodded her head. Judge Shelton stared at her and then looked down at his computer screen.

"We have received three victim impact statements. One from the widow of Detective Edward Wallace, one from Detective Debra Pedersen, and one from the mother of Carlos Arriaza. They have all waived the right to appear personally and read their statements aloud.

"Counsel," he said, looking at Leslie Westfall. "Do you waive the reading of the statements aloud."

"Yes, your Honor, as long as they remain part of the record.

"Of course," Judge Shelton responded.

Turning to the other attorney and the defendant, he said, "Counsel, does your client also waive a reading of the statements aloud or would he prefer me to do so?"

This time Hegedus stood up and responded, "My client waives the reading. He has read the statements multiple times and fully understands, and regrets, the repercussions of his actions."

"Very well," Judge Shelton continued, "I have read the pre-sentencing report and note that Mr. Moody has provided some limited assistance to the police on this matter."

Hegedus stood up abruptly. "I object to the characterization of my client's assistance as being limited. His cooperation with the Portland Police Department led to the arrest of six members of the Hoover Street Gang and he has agreed to testify should any of those cases go to trial. That should not be dismissed as merely being *limited* assistance. I request that the Court correct the record to reflect the extent of my client's full assistance with the police."

"Ms. Westfall?" asked the judge, turning to the prosecutor.

"Your Honor, I believe you were correct in characterizing the defendant's cooperation as limited. While he did provide some assistance regarding the Hoover Street Gang, he declined to assist us with information regarding the Patriot Boys, a group with which he had been affiliated for years."

"Objection!" Hegedus interjected sharply while slamming her hand on the table in front of her. "My client has consistently and expressly denied having any involvement with the Patriot Boys. He is in no way a racist and, in fact, is a twice-decorated veteran of the Afghan war, having received both a bronze star and a purple heart. Mr. Moody has been suffering the effects of his military service and has been diagnosed with PTSD, as well as depression, and is suspected of having a traumatic brain injury, as well. In addition..."

"Counsel, stop!" demanded Judge Shelton.

Hegedus stopped speaking but she still sat very straight and stared aggressively at the judge.

"I appreciate that this is the first time you've appeared in my courtroom so I'm going to cut you a little slack, but not much. In my courtroom, you don't speak unless spoken to. You don't make rambling objections. In my courtroom, you stand when I address you and whenever you respond to any of my questions or make an objection. Do you understand?"

Hegedus nodded but only responded with "yes," as she slowly rose to her feet.

"Further, counsel, when people address me, they *always* address me as 'Your Honor' or 'Judge Shelton.' Do you also understand that?"

Again, Hegedus again nodded and responded "Yes."

"Ms. Hegedus, I'm going to give you one more chance to respond to that question. If you don't answer fully and properly, I will hold you in contempt of court. Do you understand that?"

"Yes…your Honor."

"Good, now that we understand one another, I'll continue as I intended to with Ms. Westfall. Is that alright with you?"

"Yes."

"I'm sorry, I don't think I heard you. What did you say?"

"Yes, *your Honor*," Hegedus responded, barely disguising an obvious tone of disgust in her voice.

"Thank you. Now, Ms. Westfall, what evidence do you have of Mr. Moody's affiliation with the Patriot Boys?"

"Your Honor, it is well-known both in our office and in the Portland Police Department that Mr. Moody has been a key member of the Patriot Boys for over seven years, since right after his discharge from the Marines."

"So, Ms. Westfall, the fact that you represent this as 'well-known information' within the confines of your office and the Portland Police Department, means you consider it to be sufficient for my consideration? Is that accurate?"

"Of course not, your Honor, but had I known that this was going to be an issue, I would have had a representative of the Portland Police Department present to testify."

Judge Shelton looked around the courtroom and then responded, "I don't see any representative of the Portland Police Department here. Is it safe for me to assume that you'll agree that without such representative, I should ignore your representation as to Mr. Moody's affiliations?"

"Yes, your Honor," Westfall responded reluctantly.

"Very well, then I'll get back to what I was saying before this pointless interruption. I have read the pre-sentencing report, as well as the US Attorney's sentencing recommendation. Ms. Hegedus, is there anything you want to add to your prior improper argument?"

"Yes, your Honor," Hegedus said as she stood up and walked over behind her client. Placing her hands on his shoulders, she continued, "Your Honor, my client fully admits his reprehensible conduct. As much as he would like to, he wishes he could explain what caused this momentary, but completely uncharacteristic, act that deprived two people of their lives and another to suffer grievous and permanent injury. I have had to advise him, however, not to add anything further. There is no excuse for his actions, and he will accept the Court's sentence. I will remind the Court, however, that his patriotic service to this nation, as well as the long-term injuries suffered in such service, should be taken into account by the Court."

Hegedus then sat down and grasped her client's hand on top of the table.

"Very well, I'm going to keep this short. I recognize the Court's sentencing guidelines and issue the following sentence—on the first charge for the murder in the first degree of Edward Wallace, I sentence the defendant to prison for a term of not less than forty-five years with no possibility of parole. On the second charge of murder in the first degree of Carlos Arriaza, I sentence the defendant to prison for a term of not less than forty-five years with no possibility of parole. On the third charge for attempted murder of Debra Jane Pedersen, I sentence the defendant to prison for a term of not less than thirty-five years with no possibility of parole.

"On the fourth charge of manufacturing an explosive device, I sentence the defendant to prison for a term of not less than forty-four years with no possibility of parole. On the fifth and final charge of domestic terrorism, I sentence the defendant to prison for a term of not less than fifty years with no possibility of parole. All sentences will be served concurrently."

Judge Shelton put down the pad of paper he had been reading from, took off his reading glasses, and spoke directly to the defendant. "Mr. Moody, your actions in this matter are heinous and disgusting. They are completely and utterly contrary to your service as a Marine and the oath you took to uphold the Constitution of the United States.

"You have ruined countless lives, not just those directly affected, but those of the friends, family, and colleagues of your three victims, particularly those of Detectives Wallace and Pedersen.

"What is just as bad, however, is the impact that this will have on your family. I see that you are married with two young sons. Those children will never have their father to help them with their homework or teach them how to throw a baseball or drive a car.

"They will likely be teased and scorned for being the children of a convicted murderer. You have not only failed as a Marine and a citizen of this great country, but you have failed as a father. I feel no sympathy for you because whatever sympathies I may have, are directed to the victims, including your two young sons.

"Shame on you and I take a measure of pride knowing that with my sentence, you'll never have the opportunity to hurt any other innocent person. I hope you are prepared for the rest of your life as an inmate.

"Counsel, we are done. Bailiff, please ensure that the defendant is escorted to the holding cell and then transported to prison pursuant to the guidelines of the Federal Bureau of Prisons."

With that, Judge Shelton gathered his robes and began to stand.

"All rise," said the Bailiff.

Shelton then strode out of the courtroom. As the marshals walked behind the defendant and started lifting him to a standing position, Hegedus leaned over and whispered, "Tuna will stand by his promise. Your family will be taken care of."

Moody could barely lift his head and didn't have the energy to respond. Tears started running down his face, but with his hands bound behind him, he had no way of wiping them away.

Chapter Forty-One

"Bill, you seem oddly quiet. What's up?"

"I think I'm just exhausted from this case. It's been so damn frustrating. I feel like I'm missing something, but I can't figure it out. It's kind of like when you have the dream that you're trying to reach out to someone, but they are always just beyond your grasp."

Dr. Malone leaned forward in her chair, looking carefully at the man across the desk from her. He seemed different somehow.

"Do you often have that type of dream?"

"Oh, come on, Doc. A dream is just a dream. Don't read into it as anything more than that."

"Bill, sometimes a dream isn't just a dream. Sometimes it is our subconscious trying to work out some unresolved conflicts or issues. In these dreams, who are you trying to reach out to?"

Karb looked down. She could see him start to grip the armrests on his chair. His breathing increased but then she saw a change. He took a deep breath, forcing his body to relax.

"Doc, can we not do this today? I'm really frustrated and tired and I'm just not in the mood for a deep dive. Can we do that some other day?"

"Fair enough, Bill. As long as you agree that we will do the 'deep dive,' as you say, some other day, we can move on. Let's talk a bit more about the Charlene Price case. Was it difficult when you found out about Wilkerson and Davies disappearing? I thought that might…well, I thought that might be difficult for you."

"I've spent the last several nights at the gym just trying to work out the frustration from that."

"Is that the only way you've been dealing with your frustration?"

"Doc?"

She could sense some anger in his voice.

"You're right, we'll save that for another day. Old habits die hard, I guess."

"So, let's talk about another way to handle the frustration, rather than just beating up on a punching bag. Let me ask you a question."

"Okay."

"Did you do everything in your power to figure this case out?"

"Yeah."

"Is there anything you could have done to prevent Wilkerson and Davies from disappearing?"

"That's the thing, Doc. I keep telling myself that I'm missing something, but just can't figure out what. I hate that feeling. I feel like I've failed. I failed Charlene, I failed her daughter, and I failed the captain."

"Again, Bill, you did everything you could think of, right?"

Karb nodded his head.

"And neither Capobianco nor the captain were able to figure it out either, right?"

"Yeah."

"And you respect the skills of both the captain and Capobianco, right?"

"Yeah." This time, his response sounded more tired than frustrated.

"Well, then, if there was nothing else you or the others could have done, then *you* didn't fail, and no one is suggesting you did."

She leaned forward slightly. "Bill, we can only control what we can control. Whichever one of those guys killed Charlene, he was very careful about it. He must have felt the noose closing in on him. Whether it was Wilkerson running away or Davies killing himself, does it really matter?"

She waited for a response, but none was forthcoming.

"In either case, there was nothing for you to control. You're limited by the requirements of the law and criminal procedure and this one just didn't work out. That's not your fault, just like it's not Capo's fault or the captain's fault."

"I guess."

"Bill, think about it this way. Wilkerson may have a lot of money, but he'll be on the run for the rest of his life. He'll have to live in some godforsaken country that doesn't have an extradition treaty with the US, and he'll constantly be looking over his shoulder. What kind of life is that?"

Karb looked at her but didn't respond, so she continued, "Davies lost everything—his wife, his best friend, and then his life. Neither of these guys won. In fact, no one won. Charlene Price is the only victim, and we can only hope that she can rest in peace."

She looked at Karb and he was still just looking back at her.

"Bill, again, you can only control what you can control. You can't control what happens to Wilkerson, but you can control how you deal with your frustration."

'Yeah, I guess."

"Bill, it's more than just a guess. You know I'm right, don't you?"

"Yeah." His response didn't have much enthusiasm, but Dr. Malone couldn't tell if that was due to acceptance or fatigue.

Karb stood up, walked over to the window, and looked out. It was a warm late summer day, and the sun was shining brightly.

The leaves in the trees just outside the window were just starting to change from green to burnt orange. He took his time and soaked up the beauty.

Finally, he turned back to Dr. Malone and said, "Doc, I think I'll be ready to talk about Janice next time."

"Bill, good for you. I'm really proud of how far you've come. I look forward to continuing our conversation next week."

Karb walked over and shook her hand, staring into her eyes the whole time. He then turned and walked out. Dr. Malone picked up her Dictaphone and started dictating her notes.

An exciting and inspiring future awaits you beyond the noise in your mind, beyond the guilt, doubt, fear, shame, insecurity, and heaviness of the past you carry around.
—Debbie Ford

ᴄᴈ

Chapter Forty-Two

It was a perfect winter day in paradise. The temperature was in the low eighties and only a few cumulus clouds marred the azure sky. He sipped his mojito, then leaned back and looked out over the ocean. The water was calm and seemed to go on forever. He looked over at his husband and reached for his hand.

"Didn't I tell you that this place was beautiful?"

"You did. How did you hear about it?"

"Jim, you know I do my research. Melia Buena Vista is one of the finest resorts in the whole Caribbean. I knew you needed a getaway and was just waiting for the right time to bring you here."

Dr. James Matthew Davies looked out over the ocean and then at the bright white sand off to the side. He had to admit that this was truly lovely and maybe just the thing he needed in order to finally relax. The last year in particular had taken a toll on his mental health.

"How long are we staying?"

"I booked us for another ten days. If you can't completely unwind in two full weeks in this paradise, I give up."

Looking back at his husband, Davies smiled and said, "I'm pretty sure I'll be able to do that. This really is remarkable. Thank you."

"Excuse me, gentlemen, I hate to interrupt you, but I simply must."

The two men sat up and looked behind them, only to see an Asian woman and a middle-aged man walking down the dock to where they were seated.

"I don't know if you remember me, Randy, but I'm Meg Nguyen and you remember my friend here, Bill Karb."

Wilkerson stood up, his face starting to get red.

"We're not accepting visitors. Please leave immediately or I'll call security."

"Oh, Randy…or is it Christopher Lynch? In any event, we've got a little time. I convinced the manager and the waiter to give us ten minutes so we can have a little talk. I told them that I was your niece and just wanted to say hello. It wasn't inexpensive to convince him of that but, then again, I can't imagine that there is much at this resort that is. Do you mind if we have a seat?"

Without waiting for a response, Karb pulled two chairs over and placed them in front of Wilkerson and Davies. Wilkerson remained standing.

Karb and Meg sat down. Karb said, "If you don't mind, I'll refer to you as Randy, rather than Christopher or Chris or whatever other alias you might be using down here. Will that be alright?"

Neither man responded until Wilkerson said, "I don't know what you two think you're doing here. Detective, you know you have no jurisdiction here and, anyway, Cuba doesn't have an extradition treaty with the US. Meg, we're certainly not going to bother talking to you, just so you can spew it out on that bullshit podcast of yours. We'd like you to leave now."

Meg and Karb sat silently and Karb again motioned that Wilkerson should have a seat. Reluctantly he did.

"What do you want?" Wilkerson asked.

Meg responded first. "Randy, there are always a lot of things we want but we also know that life is full of disappointments. For example, Bill here was so disappointed about the thought that one of you got away with murder. I, on the other hand, never had that same level of disappointment. Quite the contrary, when I finally figured it out, I couldn't help but be impressed.

"I really have to congratulate you both. I've seen a lot of clever cons but nothing like yours. I guess your training at UW really came in handy. You both built up these amazing profiles, especially you Randy, and no one knew you were just acting very clever roles."

Davies stood up. "I'm not going to listen to this. You two need to leave!"

Karb stood and gently pushed Davies in the chest, forcing him back on to the chaise lounge.

"Dr. Davies, you don't need to listen to us, but you will," Karb said sternly.

Meg continued, "Over the course of *years*, you built relationships, set up the defective trust and then arranged for Ken Price to die on the operating table. Jimmy," Meg's voice had a taunting tone to it, "you pretty much got away with the murder of Ken Price too, didn't you? Obviously, the statement of the surgical tech Emad Aboujaoude almost screwed you over, but the Good Old Boys' Club protected you with that.

"You played this long con, knowing that with two legitimate suspects, neither of you could be convicted. Sure, there might be some civil liability, but you knew you'd be long gone before that really became a concern."

Karb stood up and reached into his jacket pocket. "That reminds me, I've been asked to serve each of you with a summons and complaint for the wrongful death lawsuit filed by Kelly Price. It might not matter to you much, but she'll get the satisfaction of at least knowing you two were served and she'll be able to get a default judgment. That will, of course, keep you from ever getting that insurance money, but I suspect you never really cared about that."

He dropped the summonses on their laps and then sat back down, turned to Meg, and nodded his head for her to continue.

Meg looked at the two men and said, "I really am curious about which of you actually killed Charlene."

Wilkerson puffed his chest just a bit and ran his hands through his long hair. "We don't have to answer any questions."

"C'mon, Randy, you don't *have* to answer this question, but I'd really like you to. We're not recording this conversation, so what do you have to lose? Even if we tried to say you confessed, it would be our word against yours and we're already trespassing, remember?"

Wilkerson looked at Davies for a moment. On one hand, he had always counseled clients to never admit to any wrongdoing but, on the other hand, he was justifiably proud of this plan, most of which had been his idea.

"Shut your phones off and give them to me."

Karb and Meg looked at one another and then Karb nodded. Both of them took their cellphones out, conspicuously turned them off, and then handed them to Wilkerson.

Before Wilkerson could speak, Meg asked, "So, Jimmy, did you put the string across the top step?"

"Ms. Nguyen," Wilkerson interjected, "don't be insulting. You will refer to my husband as Dr. Davies. If you call him anything else, we are done. Is that clear?"

"That's fair. Let me ask again—*Dr. Davies*, did you run the string across the top of the stairs?"

Davies just sat there and refused to respond. Wilkerson, however, was ready to speak. "Of course he did, it was pretty simple. It was actually a braided fishing line and he secured it across the top stair tread with duct tape. Earlier, he had placed Char's cellphone down on the kitchen counter and turned the volume as loud as it could get.

"When I got to the house, I called Char's phone. She's always been a light sleeper. We knew she would hear it. She wouldn't turn on the hall light as Jim's door was open, so she never saw the fishing line. As I was just opening the door, I heard her fall down the stairs and then saw her. It really was sad."

Karb fought the urge to reach over and throttle the smug son-of-a-bitch.

"She was still breathing, of course, and Jim insisted that I be the one to put her out of her misery. I guess he figured that we both needed our hands a little dirty." He then turned to Davies, "Isn't that right, love?"

Davies looked back at him. "Randy, do we really need to do this?"

Wilkerson reached over, grasped Davies' hand, and gave it a squeeze. Davies quickly pulled his hand away.

"Jim, we should both be proud of this. We put a lot of work, and a lot of time, into this plan. You are right, however. I won't gloat."

Turning back to their unwelcome visitors, Wilkerson said, "So that's about it. I think we are done here. Before you go, however, I'm curious as to how you found us."

"C'mon, Randy, it really isn't that difficult to find someone these days, especially someone who has embezzled over thirty million dollars. You became almost like a *Where's Waldo?* drawing. Everybody has been looking for you and I let it be known that there was a small reward for any information as to your whereabouts."

"Okay, that's fair," Wilkerson said. He seemed more than a little proud to be thought about, even if it was just notoriety. "Question two, what now? You can't arrest us, and you can't extradite us, that's one of the many benefits of living here in Cuba. Governmental officials are very loyal to wealthy foreigners."

Meg and Karb looked at each other and smiled.

CHAPTER FORTY-THREE

The Melia Buenavista resort is on a small island just off the north coast of Cuba, a five-hour drive from Havana. The island is connected to the main island of Cuba by a nearly thirty-mile causeway. The drive may be long, but Wilkerson and Davies had rented a Mercedes-Benz SL AMG Roadster. With the roof down and reggae music playing, the drive had been wonderful.

Their first week had allowed them to soak up some sun and eat gourmet food available at a wide variety of local restaurants.

What started out as the vacation of a lifetime had now taken a turn for the worse, much worse.

Wilkerson, with a cocked eyebrow, asked, "May I ask what you two find so amusing?"

Meg responded, "Of course you may, but before we discuss that, may I just say that this resort has nothing on your apartment in Havana."

Both Wilkerson and Davies stared at Meg. She thought she detected a faint flicker of alarm in Davies' eyes.

"Yes, we were at your apartment just yesterday. I've got to tell you; the view is amazing. I'd say that it's a view that only big money can buy but then, again, you didn't buy it, did you? It's my understanding that you are just leasing it. Do I have that right?"

Wilkerson leaned forward. 'You have no right to break into our home. If that is the case, we'll be contacting the police and you'll be arrested. The police don't look kindly upon burglars, especially gringos."

"Oh, Randy, you won't need to do that. We'll be out of your hair in no time. Aren't you curious as to why we were in your apartment?"

Neither Wilkerson nor Davies responded.

"Well, I would be. Wouldn't you, Bill?"

"Absolutely," he quickly responded.

"Okay, let me tell you what my thought process was. As clever as this whole con was, I suspected that you two might still make a couple of mistakes, at least I hoped you would. After all, no plan is perfect, just like no person is perfect. Combine the inherent fallibility of both of you, throw in more than your share of arrogance, and there would be mistakes. We just had to identify them…and we did. Randy, would you like to know what *your* mistake was?"

Using a smug tone to hide his increasing unease, Wilkerson responded, "Do tell."

"While it was very clever to have the trust money wired to the Cayman Islands and then to the Bank of China in Hong Kong, I was pleasantly surprised that you didn't distribute your ill-gotten gains to multiple banks in various countries. Keeping it in a single bank and even a single bank account was a bit reckless and, fortunately for me, a mistake. It made it quite a bit easier to trace. I truly expected to have to spend years trying to track your ill-gotten gains to at least a dozen banks.

"Of course, even with a single bank like the Bank of China, it would be almost impossible to access the funds without the account information and password. That then led me to wonder if your husband might have made a mistake."

Wilkerson turned sharply to Davies who simply looked back with an expression suggesting he had no idea what Meg was talking about.

"Dr. Davies, would you like to tell your husband what your mistake was?"

In response, Davies merely stared at Meg.

"Alright, let me tell him. Randy, this is not intended as an insult to your husband, but Dr. Davies has never been much of a technology buff. That's a trait he shares with my friend Bill here. I've been trying to convince Bill this whole trip that he should get a smart watch and an iPad, but he just doesn't like them. Heck, the only reason he knows how to use a computer is because he needs to for his job.

"Knowing Dr. Davies' disdain for technology, it made me think that he might have retained certain habits of the analog world. For example, I always keep my computer passwords on a piece of paper that I hide. I don't think I'm the only one who does something like that. Some of us just don't fully trust computers.

"In any event, that made me think that Dr. Davies might decide to store a copy of the bank information on something other than a computer…just in case something might happen to the computer, or you, and he needed access to the money."

She noticed that Wilkerson had again turned towards his husband and was staring. He was leaning slightly forward and Karb could see a small bead of sweat start to form on his forehead.

"If my hunch was right that Dr. Davies would keep a written copy of the bank info, I figured it would be stored somewhere at your apartment. I have too much respect for you, Dr. Davies, to think that you'd just leave it somewhere easy to find. So, Bill and I looked and looked and looked.

"By the way, congrats on the marriage. I didn't realize Cuba recognized same-sex marriages?"

Neither man responded.

"Sorry, I digress. As I was saying, we looked and looked…for hours. It was Bill who finally found it. Taping the codes to the underside of the bottom drawer of your dresser was really clever. Most people would never think to look there but, unfortunately for you, Bill Karb isn't most people."

The shock was starting to set in for both men. Davies instinctively reached over for Wilkerson's hand, but Wilkerson's hand remained stiff and didn't respond to the touch.

"Bill, I'm thirsty, do you think we have time to order a drink?"

"Sorry, Meg, but our flight leaves tonight, and we really have to get on the road soon if we're going to make it."

"Damn, that is unfortunate. Alright, gentlemen, I guess we need to wrap this up. Before we leave, however, let me just tell you that, just this morning, I wired the balance in the account." Meg hesitated and reached into her pocket. Pulling a sheet out of her pocket and looking at it, she continued, "$35,823,388.08 to the trust account of Rufus Thrower III. I left $100.00 in the account just to keep it open for you.

"Randy, I don't know if you followed what was going on with your old firm, but they were sued by Kelly Price and ended up having to pay a lot of money to her, much more than the limits on their malpractice insurance. The firm dissolved. It almost bankrupted your former partners. Rufus Thrower only survived because his wife is a successful dentist and Jada and Kehoe survived, but only barely.

"You can only imagine the relief I heard in Thrower's voice this morning when he confirmed receipt of the money. Bill, did I miss anything?"

"No, Meg, that just about summarizes where we are. The good thing for the two of you is that you're not in prison where you should be. Instead, you still have your lovely apartment, at least until the next lease payment is due."

With that, both Karb and Meg stood up.

Karb said, "It was good to catch up with the two of you and see that you're doing well. I've used up just about all of my vacation time, so I need to get back to work. If either of you are ever back in Portland, please feel free to give us a ring."

Meg turned to Karb and whispered, "Bill, I never knew you could be so snarky."

Karb softly replied, "My shrink is always telling me to try and develop new skills. She thinks it will help me build new friendships. What do you think?" He winked at her.

Karb and Meg turned and walked away, not looking back at the two now-destitute criminals. If they had, they would have seen them both staring towards the horizon, lost in their respective thoughts.

❧

Chapter Forty-Four

"Joyce, this is lovely, but I really wish you could have seen that resort in Cuba."

"Meg, I have no doubt that it was spectacular, but Manzanita is more in our budget."

They were sitting on the deck of their rental house, watching the waves as the sun slowly set.

"I love how you tied this all together in that last episode…"

Meg interrupted, "…how *we* tied this all together…"

"You're right, thank you. I love how *we* tied this all together in that last episode but there are still just a couple of things nagging at me, some loose ends."

"Like what?" Meg asked.

"Well, why did Wilkerson call you and tip you off about Charlene's death."

"Yeah, I wondered about that too. The way I figure it is that Wilkerson wanted to make sure that Davies was all in on the plan. If I hadn't started digging, the cops would have likely just written this off as an accident and Davies could still pull out and walk away and leave Wilkerson behind. While they loved each

228

other, it doesn't appear that they completely trusted one another. Maybe it was a twist on the whole 'honor amongst thieves' thing.

"Wilkerson wanted the police to investigate Char's death as a murder to ensure Davies was committed to the plan and Davies wanted Wilkerson to finish off Char to ensure *he* was committed. It's kind of fucked up, but still makes sense, I guess."

"Okay, what about the insurance policy? Davies clearly didn't need it."

"Yeah, that's one I'd like to have asked them about. I'd like to think that they had at least a tiny bit of humanity in them and knew that Kelly would get that money and be taken care of without the trust money. But then I remembered who we're talking about and suspect it was just to throw a little more suspicion on Davies and complicate the prosecution of either of them."

Joyce took a sip from her glass of Pinot Noir from the Blakeslee Vineyard and gazed back as the sunset. Both of them watched in silence as the sun slowly sank below the horizon. With a brief flash, it disappeared.

"Can I trust *you*?" Joyce asked without turning her head.

"Completely and I won't even try and convince you to murder anyone…at least not for a while."

They both turned to one another and looked into each other's eyes. After a few moments, Joyce smiled, reached over, placed her hand on Meg's forearm, and softly said, "Good."

About the Author

A lot could be said about the author but, ultimately, the question always comes down to why anything more has to be said. He's written four books so far, with more to come. Good for him. He's done a bunch of other stuff too, some interesting and some not. Who cares? He's an attorney and lives in Oregon. Blah! Blah! Blah!

His only *real* accomplishments are his relationships with his family and friends. He's been incredibly fortunate to have an amazing wife, two great children, an incredibly patient son-in-law, and two wonderful granddaughters who he adores. He's got friends who seem to recognize who and what he really is and yet still like him. He is, for the most part, happy and far more fortunate than he realizes.

> Well, I'll keep on moving,
> Moving on,
> Things are bound to be improving,
> These days.
>
> One of these days,
> These days I'll sit on cornerstones,
> And count the time in quarter tones to ten,
> My friend.
>
> Don't confront me with my failures,
> I had not forgotten them.
>
> *These Days*
> By Jackson Browne